JOURNEY INTO JEOPARDY

Former Pinkerton detective Frank Glengarry is called out of retirement to take on one final task: the delivery of a ransom to the kidnappers of Lucille Glassner, daughter of a US senator. Though assured there will be no danger, Glengarry is travelling to one of the remotest corners of California — and is about to fall foul of the law. Forced onto a trail littered with lynchings, greed, vengeance, murder and double-dealing, his only means of escape is to face up to those who want him dead . . .

MARK BANNERMAN

◆

JOURNEY INTO JEOPARDY

Complete and Unabridged

LINFORD
Leicester

First published in Great Britain in 2013 by
Robert Hale Limited
London

First Linford Edition
published 2015
by arrangement with
Robert Hale Limited
London

A catalogue record for this book is available
from the British Library.

ISBN 978–1–4448–2643–2

Published by
F. A. Thorpe (Publishing)
Anstey, Leicestershire

Set by Words & Graphics Ltd.
Anstey, Leicestershire
Printed and bound in Great Britain by
T. J. International Ltd., Padstow, Cornwall

This book is printed on acid-free paper

1

Recollection of the agony still haunted Frank Glengarry like a jagged scar in his memory. When the injury occurred he'd been working as a Pinkerton detective, just as his father had before him, and he'd been cleaning his rifle. He still couldn't explain what went wrong. He was unloading the weapon when it seemed to explode in his hands. Maybe there'd been a faulty round stuck in the breech. The blast had deafened him as the bolt was slammed back into his right hand between forefinger and thumb. He howled with revulsion but it seemed strange that there was no immediate pain, only imagined pain. But when he dared to look down at what had happened, his stomach churned.

The metal bolt was protruding from his hand like an extra finger, its base embedded between thumb and forefinger, creating a pulp of smashed bone and flesh. His thumb was hanging by no more than a thread of skin and blood was pumping out.

For a long time all he could do was slump on the ground, stunned and groaning with anguish. He felt sick, dizzy, his vision becoming a green haze, and suddenly, the agony registered. *Agony!* He'd never known anything like it. White-hot, shattering torture throbbed up his arm.

Gritting his teeth, he willed himself to extract the bolt, ripped his neckerchief from his throat and drew it about the terrible wound. After that he passed out.

Thanks to the auspices of his father's good friend, the surgeon Edward Jakes, he ended up at one of the best hospitals in New York, where the stump of what was left of his right hand, including the wrist, was amputated.

After his convalescence, he retired from the Pinkerton Agency.

* * *

While working as a Pinkerton detective, and prior to his accident, Frank had been obliged to take life. The posse, with which he'd been riding, was chasing the notorious Child-eater gang and had cornered them in an arroyo. In the confusion of the subsequent gun-battle, Frank had spotted an outlaw called Kasper Van Bremer aiming his pistol at the back of Sheriff Ollerton. Frank had fired his own gun, hitting Van Bremer in the head, killing him instantly.

* * *

When Rebecca Van Bremer discovered that it was Frank Glengarry who had killed her husband she might have been overwhelmed with hatred. But she was not. It had been much to her chagrin that her husband had been riding with the Child-eater gang. She knew he was as wicked, perhaps more so, than any of his fellow outlaws, apart from Zackary 'Child-eater' Hawkes, their leader.

Rebecca had rebuked herself for not grieving at her husband's death, but how could she when she still carried the ugly bruises he had inflicted upon her body? Several times he had threatened her with a gun, vowing to kill her if she did not yield to his bestial lust.

After his death, when fate brought her face to face with his killer, the only emotion she felt was one of gratitude. She had intense moments of feeling shame but she found respite in her religious faith — a faith that, somehow, approved of her blossoming love for Frank Glengarry. She saw that he was not by nature a man of violence, but one who had been driven by circumstance to fight the lawlessness that plagued the territory, and his terrible injury had somehow bonded them together in a happiness she had not previously known. They were married a year after meeting, and bought a small acreage of land in Marion County,

Texas, which they farmed.

In due course she converted Frank to her religious beliefs, the Hanna faith, and, apart from accepting the Lord into his life, he took on its ways, which at first seemed strange but subsequently became second nature to him: the Puritan hat, black clothes, shapeless coats with hooks and eyes instead of buttons, baggy pants and the fact that whilst forked beards were compulsory, moustaches were not allowed. The years blessed them with three children.

But fifteen years after his conversion, the past reared its ugly head; Zackary 'Child-eater' Hawkes paid them a visit at their farm. Hawkes had been the leader of the Child-eater gang, a man of the most evil reputation, who was rumoured to have committed cannibalism. He had just completed his prison sentence. On arrival he feigned friendship towards the Glengarrys, saying he had paid the penalty for his crimes. He held up a Bible, claiming he was now truly a follower of the Lord and wished to join the Hanna Church.

He was invited into the house and the three of them sat down to a meal.

But Rebecca remained suspicious and asked, 'Did thou really eat two children when thou got snowed up in the mountains?'

Hawkes laughed. 'That was just a story, my dear. Not even old Zackary was that bad.'

She didn't trust him. Her feelings were justified.

Later, when Frank was alone with Hawkes, the outlaw, truly unreformed, attempted to shoot this man who had played a part in the destruction of his gang. But Frank dodged to the side; the bullet went wide, and he fired through the pocket of his coat, killing Hawkes.

Since then, the years had flowed by, marked by hard work and contentment and strengthened by religious faith.

But when Frank was fifty-one, and his hair was turning grey, their serenity was again smashed open with a degree of violence totally unforeseen.

* * *

Lucille Glassner, daughter of the ranch owner Senator Wilber Glassner, was taking her regular morning ride across the sprawling Texas lands owned by her father. Sunlight buttered the grasslands, speckled here and there by purple wisteria, and short-horn Herefords grazed, raising their heads inquisitively as she passed. She dismounted by a river to refresh both herself and her splendid sorrel, Daisy.

Lucille was eighteen years old and already endowed with the budding beauty of womanhood. She was bright and wild-spirited, eternally smiling and happy at the prospect of her forthcoming marriage to Jim Esthelder. Now she gazed at her reflection in the water and was confident that her future husband would be proud of her. But she knew that her father disapproved of Jim, believing that not only was she too young to be a bride but also that she was betrothed to a man who was beneath her station. Particularly so, now that Senator Glassner had ambitions to become President of the United States.

However, she had remained resolute and would not be diverted from her plans, any more than he would from his.

Lucille took her pocket watch from her jodhpurs. It was 9.30 a.m. 'Time to go home,' she murmured to Daisy. 'Tutor will be arriving.' She adored the horse, treating her as an equal.

She breathed in deeply, refreshed by the air of early spring. The sky was a cloudless blue and the only sound was the sawing of hoppers' legs in the grass. She loved this spot of her father's domain, where the wandering river took a double curve. The water glinted in the sun like a field of diamonds. The current had eroded the bank, creating a cliff of red rock, and then, as if on rebound, had done the same on the opposite side. She could see a roe deer watching her from the nearby cottonwood trees.

Suddenly the animal lifted its head nervously, then darted off into the shadows.

Uneasiness touched Lucille. What had scared the animal? Even Daisy now fretted and unleashed an alarmed snort.

The girl would have been more distressed if she had known that she had been trailed, ever since leaving the ranch house.

Now she screamed as a man, swarthy and dark-skinned, appeared from the riverside rocks, his pistol raised towards her, his eyes ruthless. In that moment she knew that she could only expect brutality from this monster.

In a reckless panic she twisted around, got her foot into the stirrup and hauled herself on to the mare's back. Before she could gallop away, though, the vicious crack of the gun came and she felt an awful shudder cut through the horse. Daisy dropped like a stone and Lucille plunged with her. Fury gave her strength. She dragged herself up. She glanced momentarily at the stricken mare, unleashed a cry of horror, then hurled herself at their attacker. For a futile, hate-filled moment she bludgeoned at him with her fists, but he held her at length, his mocking laughter filling her ears. Finally, he tired of her childish rage and cracked her across the head with the barrel of his gun. She collapsed and did not rise. A trickle of blood ran from her skull, forming a tiny pool by his boot. He stooped and made sure that he had not killed her. He had other plans for her. He grunted with satisfaction as he straightened up.

2

This big man, the kidnapper, was known as Victorio. His ugly, chunky features were decorated with a deep knife-slash scar across his right cheek. His dark eyes, deep-set and predatory, had struck fear into the hearts of many.

He'd been born, one of non-identical twins, to a Mescalero Apache woman and an American father who was long gone before the birth. Victorio had been brought up, imbued with the Indian mistrust of the White-Eyes. Yet even so, he attended the school at the San Carlos Agency where he learned how to read words and to write.

When he was twenty, he became obsessed with Sonseray, the intended wife of a young Mescalero called Mattero, who was blind. So much so that he attacked Mattero with a knife, would have killed the helpless man had not another warrior intervened. In order to seek justice, Zana, the leader of the band, decreed that a fair fight would take place between Victorio and Mattero. To make the contest even, Victorio would be blindfolded. The winner would have the woman.

So the battle commenced. At first both men, in their blindness, slashed the air with their knives, much to the amusement of the onlookers. After a while, Mattero struck lucky, his blade slicing into Victorio's cheek, nigh cutting it away. Victorio went crazy. His blindfold had been pushed slightly up and he caught a view of his opponent. He sprang upon him, plunging his knife into his heart.

There were a few among the onlookers who had seen that Victorio's blindfold was no longer in place, and the word spread that he had cheated. In consequence, he was banished from the tribe. Accompanied by Sonseray, he rode away in disgrace, not even bidding his mother farewell.

His twin brother Zackary had formed his own gang of outlaws, and for two years Victorio rode with them, plundering banks and a train. But eventually the brothers fell out over Victorio's more ambitious plans. They came to blows. The fight ended with Victorio gripping his brother around the throat. He could have killed him, but, showing uncharacteristic mercy, he released him. Afterwards he regretted not finishing him off. He left the gang.

Shortly afterwards, he joined a band of Chiricahuas led by Cochise. They were 'wild' Apaches, and he took part in clashes with the US Cavalry. His proudest achievement was the slaying of an army captain, whom he beheaded before removing the scalp, which he kept attached to his belt for several years.

But one day the band's *rancheria* was attacked by the military, and soldiers torched the wickiups, killing men, women and children. Among those who died were Victorio's wife Sonseray and their baby.

He was not smitten with grief over the destruction of his family, for that sentiment was not part of his nature. What embittered him was that something he owned had been torn from his grasp.

Lusting for vengeance, he murdered a German immigrant woman while she was out gathering buffalo chips. This was followed by the slaying of three men prospecting for gold. He was never brought to justice for these killings.

Over subsequent years, he infiltrated white settlements, trading on the white side of his ancestry. He took to gathering from the prairie the sun-bleached bones of buffalo, shot down for their skins by white 'sportsmen'. These bones could be traded for onward sale to the manufacturers of glue and fertilizer. But payment was poor.

He struck up a fragile partnership with a one-handed man called Harp

Banderas, who put to Victorio the idea of kidnapping Senator Glassner's daughter and demanding a huge ransom. Victorio was attracted to the plan. Harp Banderas was familiar with the area in Texas where the Glassner ranch was located. Victorio knew that Banderas was unreliable for he lusted after women at every opportunity; he often boasted about the many rapes he'd committed. But Victorio was willing to go along with him, at least until he considered otherwise. The two plotted, gleaning all possible information about the ranch, and in particular about the habits of Lucille Glassner.

They'd agreed to split the proceeds of the ransom, taking half each.

* * *

Lucille was unconscious as Victorio gathered her up in his powerful arms and carried her through the trees to where his horse was tethered. Treating her as if she were no more than a sack

15

of grain, he threw her across his saddle, tied her firmly with rope and, leading the animal, set out to rejoin Harp Banderas. He had two ambitions: the first was to gain a ransom from one of the richest men in Texas; the second, and equally important, was to gain revenge for a deed committed many years earlier, but never forgotten, never forgiven.

Soon Lucille began to groan as her senses returned and she became aware of the awesome pain in her head.

She had been plunged into a nightmare world from which, it seemed, only death would provide relief.

★ ★ ★

At this time the President of the United States was approaching the end of his term in office and Marion County considered itself privileged to have one of its sons, Senator William Glassner, declare that, 'he had allowed his name to be put forward for nomination as the

16

Republican Party's candidate for the presidency'. Glassner's ranch was north of Travis Springs.

His campaign was well on course when the newspapers, full of details about the extreme drought in the north, also reported the sensational news that his 18-year-old daughter had disappeared. After the initial furore with no news of her return or whereabouts, the matter slipped from the public eye. Certainly Glassner would have no wish for any scandal to overshadow his ambitions of occupying the White House.

It was in July that Frank Glengarry received a letter from the Pinkerton Headquarters in Chicago. It read:

Dear Frank
Please come out of retirement for one final task. There will be no danger.

This last sentence was to prove the greatest untruth imaginable!

The letter went on to advise Frank that, if he accepted the job, he was to visit Senator Glassner at his ranch as soon as possible.

Frank agonized over his decision. He felt flattered that at fifty-one and minus a hand, his services were still in demand, but soon he censored himself for allowing such sentiments into his mind. Modesty was an embedded requirement of the Hanna Faith and by this time he had been elected a church elder and thus expected to fully uphold all its principles. Yet loyalties of the past tugged at him, and he knew that both he and his father had, during their Pinkerton service, established almost legendary status.

Rebecca was apprehensive as he read and reread the letter, and she recalled, despite the assurance to the contrary, that missions undertaken on behalf of the Pinkerton Agency had generally entailed an element of danger.

Frank prayed for guidance and after forty-eight hours of indecision, he was convinced that it was the Lord's wish that he took up the challenge. He concluded that there were reasons, other than his own interests, motivating events.

Rebecca no longer voiced objection although her eyes reflected grave concern. She would not prevent him from doing what he considered right. She embraced him with all her usual warmth and he knew that she was the only woman he would ever want.

He visited Travis Springs and sent a telegraphed message to the Pinkerton Headquarters, indicating that he would undertake the task. He would visit Senator Glassner at his ranch the next day for instructions.

He had only vague ideas of the exact nature of his proposed task, but he felt sure it would somehow involve the missing girl, Lucille.

3

By noon of the following sweltering day Frank reached Glassner's ranch. He'd heard that the senator left the running of the spread to his foreman, who hired and fired everybody from cook to wranglers, thus enabling his boss to concentrate on his political affairs. In the past Glassner had made a fortune, owning a string of banks across the southern states.

Frank found him at a corral close to the main house, watching one of his men breaking in an Appaloosa pony. Glassner was leaning on the rail, smoking a cigar. He sported a string-tie and a Stetson. He was a bull-necked, bulky man with a red face, a bushy moustache and a jaw as rigid as a horseshoe. He was expecting Frank, though he raised his eyebrows at the sight of the Hanna dress.

'We have some very important business to discuss, Mr Glengarry,' he said, reaching out to shake Frank's hand. 'But firstly, may I ask why you wear this unusual clothing?'

'I'm a member of the Hanna Church. We believe it's God's will that we dress this way and live simply.'

'I see,' Glassner nodded. 'I've never heard of the Hanna Church but I'm all for encouraging minority faiths. When I'm President I'll make damned sure you're allotted adequate funds. But I have some canvassin' to do before I get to the White House. I'm goin' on a whistle-stop tour of the nation next month. I need to expound my doctrines.'

For what seemed an age, he spoke about his aspirations, buoyed, Frank was certain, on a wave of vanity.

Finally he said, 'I believe in the value of education. Intellectual supremacy is good, physical prowess is desirable, but better than all, and without which none of us can succeed, is upright character.'

'I agree,' Frank said.

'Pinkerton told me,' Glassner said, 'that you had quite a war record before you spent ten years as a detective. It must've been a sorrowful blow to lose your hand, but no doubt it was in the service of law and order.'

Frank shook his head and explained that he had sustained his injury through his own stupidity.

The senator frowned, not impressed. He removed his hat and mopped the sweat from his brow with a large polka-dot handkerchief. He gestured towards the house. 'Let's get out o' this heat . . . and it'll be more private inside.'

The white-painted, timber ranch house was handsome, far larger than most, with brick chimneys. It boasted a broad veranda with highly polished brass facings and mounted cattle horns.

Frank followed Glassner inside, welcoming the cool shade after the blistering sun. A moment later they were seated in the study where a number of fine paintings of feathered Indians by Frederic Remington adorned the walls.

Glassner sat at his desk, putting on a pair of gold-rimmed spectacles and looking very presidential. He offered Frank a cigar and whiskey but Frank declined, gratefully accepting a glass of water instead. Glassner poured himself a generous amount of liquor, tore the wrappings from a fresh cigar and lit up. He spoke through a wreath of smoke and got straight to the point.

'As you may know, Mr Glengarry, my daughter disappeared. I've now learned she's been kidnapped. Puttin' it bluntly, I want her back. I want her back without any scandal that will damage my campaign.'

Frank nodded. 'What exactly do you need me to do?'

'I received an unsigned letter from the bastards who are holdin' her. It said they would let her go on payment of a hundred thousand dollars. It said the money must be placed in a strong leather knapsack and be delivered by ex-Pinkerton man, Frank Glengarry . . . '

'Me!' Frank exclaimed, amazed. 'How would they know me?'

Glassner continued. 'I'm as mystified as you, but they made it quite clear. They said you must come alone, and if you attempted any tricks, Lucille would be killed, and you too. They said you'd be watched through the sights of a gun.'

Frank took a deep breath and exhaled. He felt distinctly uneasy about the situation.

'Pinkerton told me there would be no danger,' he said.

'There won't be as long as you stick to the instructions. The letter said you must deliver the knapsack to the Lava Fields near Mule Lake in California. You've got to place it at the base of the big juniper tree that's at the entrance to the old Indian stronghold. You must deliver it at noon on July 31st. You've heard of the Lava Fields?'

'Of course. From all accounts it's the

most remote and forlorn place in God's creation. It's where the Indians made their stand against the army, way back in seventy-three.'

Glassner nodded and took a draw on his cigar.

Frank pondered for a moment. Having given Pinkerton assurance that he'd take the task on, he felt he couldn't pull out now, even if he'd wanted to.

'You've raised all this money?' he asked.

Glassner said, 'During my time runnin' the banks, I accumulated a whole stack of high-denomination bills. Thank God I kept them. I'm usin' them to pay the ransom. But there's somethin' I'd better tell you.'

'What's that, Senator?'

'They're all forged bills, absolutely worthless. But a layman'll never realize they're fake.' Glassner allowed himself a satisfied smile. 'I will not be bullied by criminals.'

Frank felt stunned. He'd been asked

to participate in deception. He wondered if Glassner would employ similar unscrupulous tactics if he got to be President.

'Surely this'll put your daughter at awful risk?' he said.

Glassner shook his head. 'If that were the case, I wouldn't be doin' it. Mr Glengarry, I want you to come here on July 23rd. I'll have the money ready. You'll have plenty of time to get to the Lava Fields.'

Frank nodded but he was desperately unhappy about what he was being asked to do. Then he thought of the young girl, suffering at the hands of criminals; there was no telling what they'd done to her. In fact, there was no real evidence that she was still alive.

'Do the Pinkertons know about the fake money?'

Glassner said, 'No. There's no point tellin' them. They insisted that you're not to be placed in any danger. You'll be safe back home, *with* my daughter, before the kidnappers discover they've been outsmarted. It'll be too late for them to do anythin' then.'

Questions arose in Frank's mind. With him having left the Pinkertons all those years back, why had the kidnappers insisted that he, personally, was to deliver the ransom?

And how had they known about him when he imagined himself living in apparent obscurity?

He noticed a tin-type photograph on the senator's desk. It was of a healthy-looking young girl in a frilly blouse. Standing beside her, his hand on her shoulder, was a blond man of about twenty. He was wearing a suit, which seemed too tight for his brawny body.

'Your daughter?' Frank inquired, inwardly berating himself for admiring the girl's lissom figure.

'Sure,' Glassner said. 'That's Lucille with the fella she says she wants to marry, though I'd prefer somebody more in keepin' with her station. He's just a common wheelwright, name of

Jim Esthelder. Works in Travis Springs.'

'I guess he's mighty sore about what's happened to her,' Frank commented.

Glassner sighed. 'He's made a great fuss. Keeps sending me notes, pleadin' with me to pay the ransom. Of course I'm worried about her, too, and it won't be good for my campaign if the press latches on to the case again. That's why I'm playin' along with her kidnappers — at least appearin' to.'

He took a gulp of whiskey, then went on. 'By the way, it might be a good idea if you spoke to Esthelder and tell him I'm payin' up. It'll get him off my back. Like I said, he works in Travis Springs at Carter's Wheelwrights. Don't tell him I'm usin' fake money. He wouldn't agree, so keep him thinkin' the cash is genuine. Is everythin' clear, Mr Glengarry?'

Both men stood up and Frank put his hat on.

'It's clear,' he said, but he was still deeply troubled about it.

4

Frank found Carter's Wheelwrights next to the Lucky Curse Saloon in Travis Springs. He walked through the open doorway and immediately found himself in a world of roaring furnaces, moving machinery, strips of molten metal and the deafening noise of hammering. He was approached by a rotund man in a soiled apron, obviously the proprietor.

Frank said, 'Could I have a word with Jim Esthelder, if he's here?'

The proprietor pointed towards a fellow working at the back of the shop. 'Help yourself, but don't keep him away from his work for too long.'

Frank nodded his thanks and walked between machines to where the young man paused as he was fitting a metal ring to a wheel. He was blue-eyed, handsome, bare-chested and powerful-looking. He was glistening with sweat.

'What can I do for you, sir?'

His voice was raised against the background clamour of industry and Frank realized the conversation would have to be brief.

'My name's Glengarry. I'm sure sorry to hear of the trouble you're having. I'm being employed by Senator Glassner to deliver the ransom up north.'

Jim Esthelder looked immensely relieved. 'Thank God he's decided to pay up. I just pray that no harm has come to Lucille. You see, we're gonna be married. This whole business of kidnappin' is driving me crazy.'

Frank said, 'I guess Senator Glassner wanted to put your mind at rest, so he asked me to let you know. I have to deliver the cash on the last day of the month. Lord willing, Lucille will then be released.

Esthelder wiped his brow with the back of his grimy hand. 'I'm beholden to you, Mr Glengarry.'

'I'll do my best to keep my side of the bargain,' Frank assured him.

★   ★   ★

Two weeks later, back at home, Frank shaved off his beard and hardly recognized himself in the mirror. Rebecca laughed outright and said how strange he looked, though in truth her mood was far from jovial for she dreaded the approaching day when he would leave.

That afternoon he bought himself a set of clothes — a checked shirt, denim pants, a Stetson, a bandanna and a set of sturdy boots. Obviously, travelling in Hanna garb would have attracted stares.

He wrestled with the decision of whether to arm himself or not. His first instinct was against it, that it was the Devil who was making his old interest in firearms stir inside him. But then he reminded himself that in remote areas a weapon was part of every man's apparel. It could be used to scare off mountain lions, bears, wolves and coyotes.

He went to the drawer that contained his gunbelt and his Colt.44. The last time he had fired the gun was when he had killed Zackary 'Child-eater' Hawkes. He decided he would take the gun, but he would strive his utmost not to use it on another human being. And that night he prayed that he was not starting on the slippery slope back to a life of violence which he had forsaken on marriage.

And so it was, on the appointed day, he'd left home having kissed Rebecca farewell and seen how her eyes glistened with tears. Maybe she had a premonition of what awaited him.

Later, when he called at the ranch, Glassner gave him the leather haversack containing the worthless banknotes. He had ten days to get to Northern California. There must be no mistake when it came to locating the dropping-off point.

★   ★   ★

The journey to Northern California by rail and stage had been uncomfortable and seemingly endless. Frank had guarded the cumbersome haversack with immense care, avoiding the casual companionship of fellow travellers.

Modoc Falls was the last settlement before the Lava Fields and from Fox's Livery he hired a chunky gelding with a white blaze, together with tack.

He'd asked the livery owner, Jake Fox, the way to the Lava Fields. The man had looked at him askance, but he'd provided a sketch of the route, indicating that it was some thirty miles away.

'Can't understand anybody wantin' to go to that place,' Fox commented. 'Some folks call it 'Hell with the Fires Out'.' He cocked his bald head, hoping for more information, but Frank just smiled, leaving him unenlightened.

'Another thing,' Fox went on. 'That place sure plays havoc with horses. The rocks are so sharp they cut their hoofs to shreds.'

Frank nodded.

Freshly mounted, he had followed along some twenty miles of trail without encountering another human being. Signs of the drought were everywhere. The sun was merciless and the arid land shimmered in the heat. Streams were dried up and lakes reduced to small puddles. He saw the corpses of cattle, bloated and fly-blown. He was wet with sweat and the horse lathered. Both man and animal were in need of respite.

Eventually he'd come upon a tumbled-down farmhouse. Close by were a barn with half the roof blown off, and a pole corral. The house was perched on the edge of what had once been a lake. Now it was parched dry and clogged with tules. On the other side of the house was a field that had been planted with soya, but it had all withered on the stem and was now useless stubble. Unbeknown to Frank, this was the home of the Bramptons.

He dismounted and hitched the gelding to the corral fence, then he crossed the small yard, stepped up on to the rotting boards of the veranda and knocked on the door. There was no response, but he heard raised voices from inside. He knocked again, then he heard footsteps and a giant of a woman opened up. She was maybe thirty, a veritable Amazon with broad shoulders, muscled arms and broad hips, all contained in a blue gingham dress, which looked about two sizes too small.

For a second she just glared at him and he thought she might hit him. He fancied he might have caught her in the middle of a row. But when she looked him up and down, she must have liked what she saw because her expression softened and her lips widened into a smile.

'What can I do for you, mister?' Her voice was deep and challenging.

Frank touched the brim of his hat and said, 'I was wondering if you could spare a bite to eat and a drink for a weary traveller. On repayment, of course.'

She nodded and said, 'We don't get many folks calling here. Come inside. We were just gonna have dinner. There's enough for three, I guess.'

Frank followed her into the living room. It was a complete shambles, full of scattered rubbish — bottles and cans and discarded clothes. There was also a couch with the springs poking through, a rickety, dirt-encrusted table and chairs and on the walls were numerous framed pictures of circus acrobats, white-faced clowns and animals, all hanging askew. The place stank of stale food, and a thick coating of dust adorned everything.

A grizzled little man was seated on a chair reading a newspaper. He didn't look up or greet Frank.

'He's my husband, Hector . . . Hector Brampton,' the woman said.

'Unfortunately, I now have to share his name, but take no notice of him. You can call me Blanche.'

Frank told her his name and added, 'I was wondering if my horse could have some forage and water.'

The woman called out, 'Hector, see to it!'

Her husband rose to his feet, mumbling curses. He was not much more than five feet tall and was wearing thick pebble glasses. He shuffled out through the door.

'He's the laziest man in creation,' Blanche said. 'The only thing he's ever done was to plant that field of soya beans. Now it's all dried out and useless. And he's so irritating. I mean real-awful irritating. Sometimes I think I'll kill him.'

Frank said, 'Why did you marry him, then?'

She emitted a long sigh. 'Biggest mistake I ever made. You see, I used to work for Boone's Circus. Trapeze stuff. They said I was the best catcher in the business. Heights didn't worry me. Anyway, when we were in Philadelphia, Hector came to every performance, evening and matinée, sitting in the front row. I could feel his eyes doting on me all the time. He just kept staring through those thick glasses of his. I wondered if they somehow enabled him to see through my costume, kinda stripping me naked. It was real creepy. Anyway, it so unsettled me that one night I missed my catch and Zorali, my partner, fell. Hit the sawdust with an awful thump. Died instantly.' She shrugged her big shoulders dismissively. 'They didn't reckon I was the best catcher in the business any longer. I was fired on the spot, thrown out with my baggage, which wasn't much.'

'What did you do next?' Frank asked.

'Well, I was sitting on a seat in the park, feeling like death and downright desperate, when Hector showed up. I guess he'd been following me. He told me he was very wealthy, having just inherited a fortune from his great uncle. He said if I married him, he'd buy me jewellery and fancy dresses, and we'd move out West because he owned property there. We'd have a life of milk and honey, so he claimed.' She snorted scornfully. 'And look where we ended up . . . this dump!'

Frank said, 'And what about the fortune?'

'Oh, that was just his imagination, something he'd dreamed up to tempt me. So was the talk of jewellery and posh clothes. I soon realized he was good at only one thing: telling lies. The truth is, we're as poor as church mice.' Her eyes swung to the haversack hanging from his shoulder. 'Say, Frank — if you don't mind me calling you that — what you got in that bag? Must be something awful precious for you to keep it so close.'

He hesitated, then said, 'I always bring a few necessities when I come on my journeys.'

'You can tell me,' she said. 'It'll be real confidential.'

'No.'

She pulled a face, not satisfied. But she turned away, saying, 'I best attend to the dinner, otherwise we might die of starvation.'

She went into the kitchen and he heard the rattling of pans. He waited a while and then for a reason he never knew, he followed after her and stood in the doorway watching her dishing steaming stew into bowls. She was unaware of his presence. He noticed how she spooned some powder from a jar into one of the bowls and stirred it around. *She's trying to poison me*, he thought. *She's mighty desperate to see what's in the bag.*

He stepped back into the living room and sat down at the table, his mind churning over.

She appeared a minute later, carrying three bowls on a tray. She placed them on the table, taking what seemed special care in putting a particular one in front of Frank.

'Oh,' she said, 'I forgot the spoons,'

and she went back to the kitchen.

Frank reckoned he had a chance. He exchanged his bowl for the one, he guessed, she had set for her husband. Maybe he was being sinful, but balanced against the fact that he had to deliver the ransom to get that poor Glassner girl released, he thought it would be considered a small sin.

Blanche came back with the spoons. When Hector came in a moment later, he sat at the place Frank had anticipated.

The meal consisted of chewy beef, potatoes and gravy so thick the spoon could have stood upright in it.

When they were shovelling the stew into their mouths, a grim thought came to Frank. Supposing Blanche hadn't intended to poison him, but her husband? She'd said she wanted to kill him. In that case, Frank might now be the victim. His bowl was half empty. He guessed he hadn't much option but to finish. He decided he'd pretend to be sleepy, even if he wasn't.

When the stew was eaten, Blanche produced a jug of strong black coffee and poured it into mugs. As they sipped it, Frank wasn't sure whether he felt dozy or not, but he yawned and said he was tired.

Blanche appeared full of compassion. 'You just take a rest. Why not lie on the couch and have a doze? You take that old bag off. You'll be more comfortable.'

She clutched the strap of the sack where it hung across his shoulder, but Frank pushed her away.

'No,' he said. 'I'll keep it on.' He got up, went to the couch and stretched out on it, feeling the poke of its springs. Her disappointed gaze followed him.

The fact was that he was feeling drowsy, but he was determined not to close his eyes.

Suddenly there was an almighty snore. Hector had dropped his head on to the table and was fast asleep.

Blanche came and stood over Frank. He sat up and said, 'How much do you charge for your hospitality?'

'Oh, five dollars. But maybe you could pay me in another way. Our bed's mighty comfortable and maybe I could keep you warm.'

'I'm really not cold,' Frank said.

Anger glinted from her eyes. She said, 'It gets lonely for a woman out here, 'specially when she's got a mouse for a man. And I guess you'd be mighty satisfied with me as a bedmate.'

He reached into his pocket, took out his purse and pushed five dollars into her hand.

'I'm sorry to disappoint you,' he said, 'but I'm a married man, and the Bible says, 'Thou shall not commit adultery'. I must move on. I'll leave my horse here, if you don't mind . . . on repayment, of course.'

A look of sulkiness came over her.

He put on his hat, waved his hand and went out through the doorway. He had a long trudge ahead of him.

5

If there was any more forlorn place in the world, then Frank prayed that the Lord would never send him there. There hung over the awesome landscape a strange, sinister air. On first impressions it appeared to be devoid of all life apart from a lonely black crow that flapped overhead, cawing before distance quieted it. But then he recalled that the note to Glassner had threatened that he would be watched . . . through the sights of a gun. The thought was not reassuring.

And now he'd made it to the tall bluff known as Cullen's Ridge, which overlooked the Lava Fields. He'd arrived late in the afternoon and the heat was beginning to slacken.

It was the day before that on which he'd been instructed to deposit the ransom. Beneath him stretched the age-scarred, volcanic landscape of razor-sharp rocks, deep chasms, up-thrusting buttes and shadowy ravines. The area, he had read, was some fifty miles square. On its eastern fringe, a range of shadowy mountains loomed purple against the sky. He was inclined to think that every inch of this grim region harboured some hidden danger.

In 1872 the Indians had made their stand against the US Army, a stand that had brought about the death of General Clayton and ended with the hanging of the defiant chiefs. Now only ghosts and memories remained.

But today it was not the past that concerned Frank. It was the crescent of rocks that showed some two miles away across the Lava Fields. The crescent, he had read, was a catacomb of caves, sacred to the Indians and used by them as their stronghold and refuge during the fighting.

The giant western juniper tree with its twisted trunk, standing proud at the entrance to the stronghold, was unmistakable. It was at its base that Frank was to place the money.

He glanced around the great saucer of land, seeing how desolate it appeared in the dusky light. He fancied that there were hundreds of places from which an unseen observer might have his gun trained on him. The thought made his spine tingle. He suspected that any imprudent move on his part would result in him falling foul of a bullet. The fear was in him that even if he delivered the money as instructed, it was still possible that he would be murdered. Those who had carried out the kidnapping were plainly quite ruthless. He strained his eyes, wondering if he might catch sight of some movement but there was nothing.

He mouthed a prayer for fortitude and descended a steep pathway that led down the face of the bluff, trampled by soldiers many years ago. The crunching sound of his boots seemed thunderous in the graveyard silence.

It was a night and a morning before he needed to make his way to the juniper tree; in the meantime he decided to lay low. He found himself a small cave, settled into it, partially consumed the food that he'd brought from town and took a rationed drink from his canteen. Sprawled on his belly he combed the terrain inch by inch through his field-glasses. Still there was no sign of any surveillance he might be under.

After a while weariness caught up with him, he pulled his hat over his face and, using the haversack as a pillow, he made himself as comfortable as possible on his bed of rocks, laying back and closing his eyes.

He wished he was at home with Rebecca. Knowing that she was his wife made him realize how blessed he was. He longed for the morrow to be over so that his task would be completed and he could commence his return journey, hopefully with Lucille. But right now he felt immensely lonely, despite the fact that company might be closer than he would choose.

It was — but not in the form he was suspecting.

He slept for longer than he'd intended. When he came awake he was aware that night had fallen and the air had cooled considerably. His bones felt stiff. Maybe he was getting too old for this sort of work.

He wondered if anybody who was spying on him would allow themselves to relax their vigil during the hours of darkness. He said his prayers. He no longer felt sleepy. He imagined that the night would prove long and chilling. Afterwards there would just be the morning to get through.

He guessed it would take him an hour to scramble across those rocks to the juniper tree and rid himself of the worthless burden, which he'd borne across half the continent. On second thoughts it wasn't worthless; it was the price of a young girl's freedom. One thing was certain: he would need no second invitation to quit this miserable place.

But his planning was to no avail.

As he pushed himself to his feet, a rattle sounded, filling the cave with angry, vibrating sonance. In the faint glimmer of moonlight, he glimpsed movement close by, and with it came the fetid scent of a snake's anger. It had clearly shared his resting place, lulled by his body heat, but now it was as awake as he was. He could just distinguish its spade-shaped head weaving, its tongue spitting probingly into space. It reared, and he staggered back, but he was too late. Three feet of malignity rocketed into him. Agony sharp as a knife thrust stabbed into his right arm just above the amputation. He forced himself to look at the wound. He saw the bead of blood, showing darkly, that stood proud for a brief moment before dripping downward.

The snake had withdrawn, slithering into the shadows, leaving him reeling with shock as foreboding coiled in his belly. He recalled that he'd once heard a doctor advise that the only way to relieve the pain was to carve the flesh through to the bone.

In desperation he reached into his pocket and withdrew his small knife. Gritting his teeth he stabbed its point several times around the bite but he failed to cut deep.

He pressed his lips to the wounds, striving to draw out the poisoned blood and spit it away, but his weakness seemed to have deprived him of the ability to suck.

He changed tactics. He removed his neckerchief, knowing that he must fashion a ligature before blood and lymph carried venom through his body. He drew it around his arm and, using teeth and trembling fingers, knotted it tight. Even so, his arm was encased with pain and his elbow was swelling.

He tried to move but a slow and heavy coldness was spreading through his body.

He lowered himself to the ground and all at once the fear was in him that the snake might not be alone. Maybe the cave concealed a nest of them! He felt light-headed; his brain was spinning. The knowledge that he had slept with a dormant rattlesnake as his bedmate was daunting.

His breathing had become shallow, as if a wheelwright's metal band was encircling his chest; despite the darkness his vision was turning into a yellow blur. He groaned, feeling the desperate need to vomit but capable only of slumping back against the haversack.

He knew western diamondbacks had the reputation of paralyzing their victims only to return later to feed. Once he lost his grip on his senses, would he ever regain consciousness?

6

Jake Fox's wife, Margaret, always said he could never make his mind up, that he wavered this way and that. But Jake didn't agree. He said he ran an unwaveringly good business — Fox's Livery in Modoc Falls, which he owned.

Now, in the town's cemetery, he and Margaret stood by an open grave and watched as their daughter Carolyn's coffin was lowered down. She'd been just seventeen.

Jake was a bald-headed and bespectacled man. His left leg was withered. He had sustained the injury as a child, when his horse stepped into a gopher hole and went down. Jake was crushed underneath and crippled for life.

His wife, plump and homely, held his arm, seeking support.

The minister was speaking soothing

words: 'And the peace of God, which surpasses all understanding, will guard your hearts and your minds in Christ Jesus.' The gathering of townsfolk listened intently but the Foxes hardly heard because they were too choked with emotion. Shortly, as the minister murmured, 'Earth to earth, ashes to ashes,' Jake's face became contorted. He was trembling with hatred. He would not rest until the fiend responsible for his daughter's death faced justice!

If he closed his eyes, the whole nightmare of the tragedy became vivid to him. It had been nearing midnight a week ago, and he'd been about to close down the livery. The stranger had ridden in and asked to stable his mount and give it a feed of grain. Having turned off his oil lamps prior to locking up, Jake didn't get a clear view of the man's face. At first, all he could see was the burly outline of his figure as he swung from his saddle, and he caught the taint of whiskey on his breath.

'Sure, I can take your horse in,' Jake said. 'Payment in advance. Three dollars for the night.'

The stranger grunted agreement, and paid. 'There's somethin' else,' he said. 'I'd like to bed down in the straw, alongside the horse. I gotta get away early in the mornin'.'

Jake felt uncertain. There was something intimidating about the stranger but at least, if he was a horse thief, there were no animals in the livery worth stealing. After a moment he nodded. 'Won't object to that. Close the livery door when you leave.'

'Sure,' the man nodded.

Jake went to unsaddle the animal, but the stranger prevented him, saying, 'Don't. I'll just loosen the cinch. I'll be leavin' in a few hours.'

It was now Jake noticed that the man had his left hand missing, although he seemed quite adept and it probably wouldn't inhibit the use of his gun, holstered on his right hip.

Finally he said, 'Suit yourself then,'

and hauled out a sack of oats. Then he left the man and limped along the deserted street towards his home, two blocks away. He hoped Margaret had left supper out for him.

Suddenly his foot caught on a rut and he fell on to the hardened mud, face first. For a moment he was stunned, but as his senses cleared he felt pain in his crippled leg. With great effort he forced himself to his feet and, grinding his teeth with anguish, he continued homeward.

Margaret and Carolyn had gone to bed, but there was a supper of sausage, potatoes and cornbread on the kitchen table, together with a glass of buttermilk. As he ate, the pain in his leg seemed to increase. He felt it, wondering if it was broken. He reckoned he would send for the doctor in the morning.

After a restless night, Margaret set off to leave a message for Doctor Crabtree. She told Jake, who was still in bed, that she had sent Carolyn to open up the livery in case there were any early customers.

Later the doctor came and examined Jake, assuring him that he had no broken bones, just a bad sprain. He should rest for a while, keep off the leg. After the doctor had departed, Margaret said she would go to the livery, taking some breakfast for Carolyn.

When she reached the stables she sensed something was wrong. Stepping inside, she heard a strange sobbing sound. It came from one of the stalls. She rushed to it and screamed in horror.

Carolyn was sprawled amid the straw, nigh on naked, with her dress ripped away and bruises darkening her pale skin. Unmistakable teeth marks were etched into her neck. There was a gash on her forehead and blood was trickling down her cheek. Deep shudders convulsed her body. When she turned her eyes on her mother, Margaret glimpsed total despair.

'Mother . . . he r-raped me!' the girl

groaned. Margaret died a thousand deaths.

'*Oh, God!*'

She went to her daughter, knelt down in the straw at her side. 'Who did it?' she gasped.

The girl had difficulty forming the words, her lips quivering, but at last she managed it.

'The m-man with one hand,' she sobbed.

Margaret cried with anguish.

After a moment she left the girl and called to the blacksmith, Mr Rainbolt, who was on his way to work. He rushed to her aid, gathered Carolyn in his muscular arms and carried her back to the house. He helped put her to bed and then went to fetch the doctor. Jake was soon up, his bad leg forgotten.

Over the next days the girl's condition deteriorated. She made no attempt to communicate or leave her bed. She had no appetite for food. Her face was chalk-white. Blankness remained in her once lively eyes, the pupils dilated, and she showed not a glimmer of recognition when her parents or the doctor entered the room.

Doctor Crabtree tried to reassure Jake and Margaret, saying there was a good chance of recovery after a period of time.

But all efforts were to no avail. On the fourth day after the attack, when her mother was hanging up washing in the garden and her father was at the livery, Carolyn rose from her bed and went down the stairs and into the kitchen. Her father kept an old Colt Peacemaker in a drawer. She lifted it out, and found a box of bullets. Her fingers were trembling as she slipped one into the chamber of the gun and thumbed back the hammer. She pushed the muzzle between her lips as deep as it would go.

Then she pulled the trigger.

★   ★   ★

Frank's shadowy world drifted into shape. He was covered in a feverish sweat and sprawled on hard rock. The impression that he'd only been dreaming came to him in a swelter of relief. Dreaming not of the snake, for that had been sure-fire reality, but of a human intruder to the cave. It had been so vivid, so crazy . . . and so impossible.

He tried to move; pain throbbed up his arm and his whole body ached. He was still in the cave. God only knew how much time had elapsed, although it was still night for he could see bright rhinestone stars speckled across the canopy of sky, revealed through the cave opening.

His mind swung back to the snake and he groaned. *The bite!* He touched it and felt the swelling. The tourniquet was still in place, but it was damp and he knew the wound was seeping blood. He was in dire need of medical attention — and there was something else: where was the snake now? He shifted uneasily, wondering if he had the strength to escape from the cave and get back to human habitation.

The dream still pounded in his head: the shuffling of feet as somebody approached; somebody in boots. Frank had grown tense. He'd tried to gather his strength and break out of the nightmare, but the fever burned in him. And then, looming in the cave's entrance, was the shadowy-black figure, silhouetted against the sky, posing an immediate threat.

He felt hands take hold of him, strong, clawing hands, dragging him to the side . . . and then the stranger had disappeared from the dream.

It had seemed much later when Frank's tortured senses resurfaced to tangibility . . . and relief seeped into his brain. Just a dream.

An urgency to move came upon him. He tried to force himself up but his weakness still persisted. As he fell back his stomach cramped and vomit erupted, half choking him. His pain was still severe and he loosened the tourniquet.

A new fear touched him. With venom in his blood, would he have enough strength to deliver the haversack to the juniper tree?

The haversack! Where was it? He fumbled around desperately, dismay growing in him. It was gone!

The dream hadn't been a dream at all. Somebody must have watched, scarcely believing their luck that he had succumbed to snakebite. They had stolen the ransom!

7

Fury gave him the energy to scramble to his feet. He swayed but after a moment his balance was restored. He moved to the mouth of the cave. Dawn was painting the far-off mountains with pink light, but the Lava Fields were still shrouded by mist. He strained his eyes, attempting to find some hint of life, but the familiar, ghostly stillness prevailed.

How long had it been since the haversack was stolen . . . and who was the thief? He was probably miles away by now. He must have kept himself hidden while he trailed Frank. His suspicions swung towards Hector Brampton. Maybe he wasn't such a dismissible character after all. Maybe now he was rejoicing at a seemingly amazing change in his fortunes. Eventually, though, he would discover his gain was worthless.

Frank knew that sooner or later he would have to confront Brampton, but now he was feeling utterly wretched. He would be unable to deliver the ransom to the juniper tree — and then what would be the fate of the girl Lucille? Steeped in his failure, only his religious sentiments prevented him from extreme profanities right then. Instead, he knelt down and prayed that he would find a way out of his predicament.

If the effect of the snake's poison allowed him, he would have to walk back to the Bramptons' farm. However, he was currently in no condition to become entangled with them again. Hopefully, his horse would still be in their corral. He would retrieve it, ride to Modoc Falls and find a doctor to give him some anti-venom, then he would send a telegraphed message to Wilber Glassner, informing him of what had happened and requesting further instructions.

Taking a final glance around and seeing nothing untoward, he cautiously set his legs in motion. Soon he was on the path that led to the ridge above. He was thankful that the day's heat had not yet risen. Pain still throbbed in his arm but as he proceeded, stopping frequently for respite, he felt his strength returning. Even so, he had to get to a doctor, preferably before he dropped dead.

It was a long and torturous walk to the Bramptons' farm and he encountered no other persons on the way. The sun was well up by the time he saw the ramshackle buildings ahead of him and sweat had rendered his clothes sodden.

On approaching, he saw no sign of life. This suited him fine. His spirits lifted when he spotted that his gelding and tack were still in the corral. Fearing that the Bramptons might suddenly appear, brandishing weapons, he climbed over the corral fence. The horse made no effort to avoid him and seemed to welcome his arrival. With some effort, he got the saddle on and tightened the cinch, then he hauled himself up on to the animal's back. He was still feeling dizzy and weak. He didn't linger. Glancing anxiously over his shoulder, he quit the farm and headed for town. The trail led between high banks clothed with mesquite.

It was an hour later that a gun blasted off and lead, like an angry hornet, whined close to his head.

The gelding reared, nearly throwing him, but he calmed him. He sat for a moment, reined in, in the middle of the trail, knowing he was now a perfect target. He braced himself for a second shot, but it didn't come. Instead a couple of strangers emerged from their cover, blocking his way, their rifles levelled at him.

Unbeknown to him, these were the Hudspeth brothers.

Seth Hudspeth, the taller of the two, was scrawny-thin and wearing a black hat. His narrow face was a mess of pockmarks. Silas Hudspeth was grinning, displaying ruined yellow stumps for teeth. He appeared to have only one eyebrow. The clothing of both men was shabby.

'It's the doggone sonovabitch for sure,' Seth proclaimed, gesturing with his gun. 'Raise your arms and don't try no fancy tricks!'

Frank saw no sense in arguing with these two itchy-fingered ruffians. He lifted his arms.

He forced himself to be calm. 'Why are you doing this?'

Silas Hudspeth spat words out through his moustache. 'You know damn well, so don't try bluffin'. We heard you was lingerin' in these parts and we know the law has put a nice fat reward on your head. So's we're gonna hand you over to Marshal Colpett. I'm sure he'll fix a neat little hangin' for you.'

His brother spoke out the side of his mouth. 'Keep him covered, Silas. I'll fetch the horses. 'If he tries anythin' fancy, plug him!'

'That'll sure be a pleasure,' Silas responded as Seth disappeared into

66

the trees. He returned a moment later leading a couple of bone-poking mounts.

Frank was getting impatient. His snake-bitten arm was aching badly, particularly as it was held up. 'Hold on,' he said, 'whoever you think I am, I'm not him.'

The other two had mounted up, keeping their rifles pointed at him.

'Button your lip, mister,' Seth snarled. 'Save your explainin' for Marshal Colpett. He won't take kindly to your lies. Now get movin'.'

Frank lowered his arms. Seth edged ahead, leading the way, while his brother brought up the rear.

As the little cavalcade headed for Modoc Falls, Frank had no option but to string along with the mean-faced pair. He intended to go to town anyway and he figured he would soon sort things out with the marshal. He hadn't a clue whom he had been mistaken for, but whoever it was, with a reward on his head, he must be awesome.

A half-hour's fast trot brought them into town. Passers-by glared at them from the sidewalks. A group of women pointed at Frank and screamed bitter insults, calling him a filthy animal. Several men even spat in his direction. He felt as if he was running a gauntlet. Shortly, a mob was following along behind as well: women, men, children and dogs. Everybody seemed to be shouting curses and waving their fists.

The hounded trio reached the marshal's office at the end of the main street. The brothers dismounted, making Frank do likewise. They hitched their animals to the rail.

A worried-looking man stepped out from the office. He was wearing a black string-tie and a nickel star was pinned to his shirt. His lean, middle-aged face was dominated by severe brows. A heavy Colt hung from the cartridge belt that circled his hips. His umber eyes flicked over the gathered mob, and he quieted them with a held-up hand.

'Go home,' he commanded. 'This

ain't no place for a meetin'.'

Almost meekly folks backtracked, melting away, but not before a man cried out, 'We want justice, Marshal. There's been too much pussy-footin' around in the past.' Several shouts of agreement sounded.

Marshal Harry Colpett had once been known as a town-tamer, a hard man, but recently his good name had become somewhat tarnished due to the fact that he seemed to be favouring local farmers above the townsfolk. Of course, the disastrous drought, that showed no signs of relenting, had left everybody tetchy and exasperated.

Colpett had gambled on a ploy he hoped would restore his reputation. He knew of a fellow, William 'Cloudbuster' Ketchum from Boston, who was said to have miraculous powers over natural phenomena.

In short, he was a rainmaker. Colpett had heard he had achieved success in Arkansas, bringing on a shower. He'd put to local farmers the proposition of bringing Ketchum to this corner of California to work his magic, and the farmers agreed that anything was worth trying because they were losing big money in dying cattle and crops. But Ketchum didn't come cheap. He demanded his huge fee whether he proved successful or not. Most of the farmers were taken aback when the exorbitant sum was revealed, but to Colpett's surprise they stomped up half the fee, saying the balance would be paid if the rain came.

However, the marshal was given a stark warning. If the scheme failed, he would be removed from office.

But right now his attention had switched to other matters.

He faced the Hudspeth brothers and said, 'What've you two rogues brought in?'

'We found him skulkin' outside of town,' Seth Hudspeth explained. 'We kinda figured you might pay out that reward for capturin' the sonovabitch.'

The marshal eyed Frank, his gaze

taking in the fact that his hand was missing.

'The bastard that raped Jake Fox's gal,' Silas announced triumphantly.

Frank exploded with indignation. 'I did no such thing!'

'Of course you'd say that, you scum,' Seth sneered. He turned towards Colpett. 'How about the reward, Marshal?'

'You'll be rewarded if he stands trial and is found guilty,' the marshal said.

'I guess we could have an advance?'

'No,' Colpett responded firmly. 'Now bring him inside. We'll get him locked up.'

Frank's anger was rising. 'Hold on. This is crazy. What exactly am I supposed to have done?'

There was a stunned silence. It was as if speaking words that would adequately describe the evil deed was beyond normal capability.

Eventually the marshal spoke. 'It was so awful the poor girl shot herself. It was just as bad as if you'd killed her yourself. Now let's get you locked up, like I said.'

Frank was propelled forward with a shove from Silas's rifle butt. The marshal led the way into the office; at the rear end was a cell.

Seth said, 'That gal's daddy sure gonna be grateful when he finds out we got the sonovabitch locked up.'

Frank was bundled behind bars. The heavy key grated as it was turned in the lock.

8

Frank sighed with exasperation. His arm was still throbbing painfully and his head was muzzy. Gazing through the bars he saw that Marshal Colpett was busy writing something. When he finished he handed it to Seth Hudspeth.

'That's a receipt for this fella.'

'What about the reward?' Seth inquired again.

'Like I told you, you'll get it if he's found guilty,' the marshal responded. 'Where can you be contacted?'

'The Golden Rooster Saloon,' Seth said. 'How do we know the law'll play square with us? I don't trust the law.'

'You got your receipt,' Colpett said. 'Don't lose it. You'll get the money if — '

'*When* he's found guilty.' Seth finished the sentence.

The marshal nodded.

The two brothers grunted, as if to seal the deal, then, muttering, they left.

'Marshal,' Frank called through the bars, 'I haven't raped anybody. I'm not the fella you want. I may be missing a hand, but there the resemblance ends. And there's something else. I'm not feeling too well right now. I got bitten by a rattlesnake. I need medical attention.'

Colpett eyed him suspiciously, but Frank held up his stump of an arm, showed him the ugly swelling.

'God a'mighty!' Colpett exclaimed. 'Snake bit, eh? Well, I'll let Doc Briggs know. He may decide to visit you.'

Frank nodded. 'Look here. I'm working for the Pinkerton Detective Agency. You can telegraph the head office in Chicago. They'll put you right.'

Colpett sniffed doubtfully, but he said, 'When my deputy takes over here, I'll do just that. Mebbe it'll call your bluff.'

Frank slumped down on the wooden bunk. He was filled with frustration.

Everything had gone wrong with his mission. He'd been coerced into taking part in deception. He'd got mixed up with a crazy farmer and his even crazier wife. He'd been attacked by a venomous serpent. He'd failed in his mission to deliver the ransom. And he'd been waylaid by a couple of greedy ruffians and handed over to the law, accused of a crime he hadn't committed.

He guessed the Lord was testing him in some way.

Twenty minutes later, Deputy Buller came in for his stint of duty. Buller looked little more than a boy. He had large buckteeth. He listened incredulously as Colpett filled him in on the situation, taking glances in Frank's direction. Afterwards, the marshal left and he must have got a message to the doctor, because within ten minutes the medical man arrived, clutching his bag of instruments and potions. He was a heavy-jowled, bespectacled man with long bushy sideburns and a complexion that implied high blood pressure. He was let into Frank's cell, a scowl on his face.

'So you're the monster who abused that sweet girl?'

Frank shook his head. 'Not me.' He felt too unwell to give further explanation.

Doctor Briggs grunted, then made a perfunctory examination of Frank's arm. He had little stomach for treating criminals, particularly when they deserved a death sentence, but he always adhered to his Hippocratic oath and now was no different. He'd come prepared.

He reached into his bag and extracted a glass tube with a plunger at one end and an evil, bayonet-like needle at the other. He removed the plunger from the cylinder, then produced a small bottle and poured its thick contents into the cylinder. 'Antivenom serum,' he explained. 'It'll either kill you or cure you. The needle won't hurt as much as the snake bite — not quite.'

He replaced the plunger on the

cylinder and told Frank to hold out the stump of his arm.

Frank felt a sharp stab of pain as the needle was jabbed home and the serum forced into him.

Afterwards, with a small knife, Briggs made several cuts around the bite, to allow it to drain. Frank clenched his teeth to avoid complaining. Next, the doctor sponged a solution of permanganate of potash on to the wound, finally bandaging the arm. Considering his disdain for Frank, the doctor's touch had been surprisingly gentle.

'I guess you'll live,' he said. 'At least for the time being.'

'I'm real grateful, Doc,' Frank said. 'I'll remember you in my prayers.'

Briggs closed his bag. 'You better remember yourself first and beg forgiveness.'

Frank nodded and thanked him for the injection, then Deputy Buller let the doctor out of the cell and he was gone.

Frank slumped back on the wooden bunk, feeling as helpless as a tied-up hog. But not for long because his thoughts swung to Rebecca and all the inspiration she had given him, and he told himself he must keep the faith.

That faith was sorely tested an hour later when Marshal Colpett returned and, leaning against the cell bars, said, 'I been over to the telegraph office, but you're out of luck. The lines are down. May be a week or so before they're restored. You'll just have to sweat it out and maybe meditate on your sins.'

Frank sighed with frustration. 'Surely there's somebody around here who would know I'm not the rapist.'

'Only the girl's father, and the last I heard he's outa town. Young Carolyn would know you, all right, but she's in her grave. God rest her soul.'

The night settled in. Frank lay on his bunk. It seemed harder than the rock on which he'd passed the previous night, but at least there were no rattlesnakes to keep him company, and he did manage to sleep.

Dawn came and the long, dreary

hours of the next day dragged along, punctuated only by mealtimes, trips to the privy and the changeover of duties for the lawmen.

At ten o'clock that evening, Colpett again completed a stint of duty. The two deputies took over: young Buller and an older man, Brad Feleen, who had a gentle voice but looked as tough as leather. Before he left, Colpett said, 'I'll take the keys to the cell home with me. If anybody comes here and tries to get him out, they'll have me to reckon with.'

With Frank's second night of incarceration taking hold, oil lamps were lit in the office.

He attempted to pacify his concerns with the hope that soon the matter of his identity would be resolved and he would be freed. It was regrettable that the telegraph system was out of action but maybe it was operating in another town that was not too far away. He wondered what Glassner's reaction would be when he learned that the ransom had been stolen. The fact that he had failed in his allotted task depressed him.

Presently he could hear the subdued voices of the deputies as they conversed over their coffee. Straining his ears, he caught the mention of somebody called Ben Hardwright and of vigilantes, and of the fact that there was a crowd getting liquored up in the saloon. After a while the conversation died out and Frank could glean no further information. Frustrated that there was nothing he could do to ease his predicament, he closed his eyes and dozed off.

He was roused by shouting from outside in the street. Drunkards! he thought. He heard the soft voice of Deputy Feleen mouthing gentle curses. He rose from his bunk and peered through the cell bars. The voices from outside had grown louder.

Deputy Buller's anxious words came, strangely high-pitched. 'There's trouble for sure. Mebbe one of us ought to fetch the marshal. He'd sort 'em out.'

Feleen said, 'We'd never get through that mob. They're fired up with liquor.'

Suddenly a single and powerful voice rose above the others from outside. 'We want the rapist. Give him over and there'll be no more trouble.'

Frank felt a chill cut through his veins. With his lone hand, he tugged at the bars and found them unyielding. He felt like a caged beast. He sensed that the mob in the street was pressing forward — a tide of murderous lust. If they got their hands on him, there would be no chance of arguing his true identity. He'd be dragged to the nearest tree and a noose looped around his neck.

'Bolt the door!' Deputy Feleen shouted and his younger partner hurried over to the outside door and slid the bolt across.

Within seconds there was a thunderous pounding of angry fists against the door, and somebody smashed its glass,

81

which shattered inwards on to the floor. All at once the racket grew silent and the same powerful voice that had called previously sounded again.

'Open up, by order of the Modoc Falls Vigilantes!'

Then the shouting started again.

Young Buller stepped across the room and faced Frank through the bars. His face was as white as alabaster. 'We won't be able to hold 'em off for long,' he said, strangely apologetic.

'You could let me out of this cell,' Frank said.

'I don't have the key,' Buller said.

He turned away as heavy kicks slammed against the door. A moment later it burst inward, the bolt busted. Men surged into the office. At their head was a tall man with a long black beard. He was clad in high boots and a rawhide jacket and was obviously Hardwright. He seemed to be a head taller than anybody else and his beanpole body somehow produced a deep voice that carried above others and drew unquestionable respect from them.

The two deputies were protesting. Feleen shouted, 'This is against the law. You'll be punished for this!'

'The vigilantes *are* the law in Modoc Falls,' Hardwright cried. 'We're the only folk that will see that true justice is enforced.'

The deputies didn't draw their weapons, knowing that they would be hopelessly outgunned if they did. They were pushed against the side wall.

Frank could see that Hardwright was not drunk like the others. There was a sober and deadly determination about him.

With nowhere to hide in the cell, Frank retreated to the far wall and stood resolutely. Before him, pressed against the bars, were the faces of angry men, reddened by the liquor they had consumed. They were like a pack of wolves, baying for his blood.

'Get the key!' Hardwright's order briefly stemmed their shouting.

Frank was now completely resigned to imminent death; his overwhelming regret was that he would not see his beloved Rebecca again — not until they were together in the next world.

9

Two days earlier Jake Fox had become gravely concerned about his wife, Margaret. Previously, she had always had the brightest of dispositions but now, with the loss of her daughter, who had been despoiled by the most wicked of men, she had plunged into depression. She remained in her bed, weeping inconsolably. Of course, Jake grieved too, but his grief shared space in his mind with blind hatred for the one-handed monster who had brought such tragedy to their small family. He wanted him dead; nothing would change that.

But in her hopeless despair, Margaret was negative. 'How can you find that brute? You wouldn't know him if you saw him. You didn't even see his face.'

'But I saw he had a hand missin'.'

Margaret breathed in with a shuddering sigh. She knew Jake was helpless.

How could he achieve anything with his crippled leg and his lack of ability to recognize the rapist?

'When Ben Hardwright heard what had happened,' Jake continued, 'he went crazy and swore blind that he'd find the sonovabitch and lynch him.'

There was a moment's pause, then Jake's tone changed. 'Honey, I'm worried about you. We've somehow got to live through our sorrow. We've got to find strength. I think we'd best visit your sister in Jefferson City. The change of air, and seeing her, will do you good.'

'Jake, I don't feel well enough to travel. It's a day and a half's journey . . . and you know how uncomfortable the coaches are.'

He said, 'It'll buck you up to get out of this place for maybe a week. I'll close the livery down. We can stop overnight at a relay station. I'm told they provide good accommodation.'

Still she protested, but he insisted and finally, and begrudgingly, she conceded to him.

They took the early-morning stage the next day. Climbing aboard, she would have fallen had he not supported her. Of course, she was right about the coach. It was anything but luxurious. Its canvas side curtains were pinned down, yet the dust still wafted in, feeling like powdered glass between the teeth. The seats were of unsprung wood. The seven passengers were bounced this way and that as they trundled over potholes and stones and swung around curves.

Mid-morning, when they stopped at the trailside to stretch their legs, Margaret vomited and turned so pale that Jake wondered if she was dying. But reluctantly she found the strength to reboard the coach and they were soon rolling on. Jake comforted her as best he could, but gradually he had to admit to himself that taking on the journey had been a mistake.

At noon they stopped for further respite but this time she felt too ill to leave her seat. She sat, head slumped, as they started off again. Finally, after an exhausting afternoon, they pulled into the relay station. Once there, Margaret refused food and went straight to bed. Fortunately, she was the only female passenger and she had a room to herself.

Jake took supper with the rest of the passengers. It was a good meal of beef, potatoes and gravy but he, too, lacked appetite, and he was in no mood to join in the banter and general conversation. More and more he cursed himself for ever suggesting that they take the trip.

That night he watched over his wife, seeing how she twisted and turned in the bed, seemingly tortured by her dreams. Several times she called out Carolyn's name.

Should he admit defeat and take her home? After thinking about it, he reckoned it would be best to complete the journey to her sister. It was a shorter distance than that of returning to Modoc Falls.

When the stage rolled on towards

Jefferson City the next morning, they weren't on it. Margaret was still unwell and remained in bed. She gripped her husband's sleeve and said, 'Let's go home, Jake. That's the place I want to be. I'll feel better there.'

'Well, you best stay restin' this mornin',' he said. 'We'll see how you feel later.'

He was still sure there would be less stress for her if they continued to her sister's. And there was a good doctor there.

Yes, he concluded, best to go on to Jefferson.

★   ★   ★

Hardwright roared at the deputies who were pushed against the office wall. 'Hand over the cell key and nobody'll get hurt . . . apart from this rapist!'

There was a lull in the racket as the mob awaited a response. The air was tainted with whiskey fumes.

Deputy Feleen spoke in his gentle

voice. 'We don't have the key.'

'Don't lie,' Hardwright cried. 'Where is it?'

'I told you,' Feleen said calmly. 'We don't have the key.'

A gun was rammed into the deputy's chest but he didn't flinch.

Somebody grabbed young Buller by the arm and shook him. 'Where's the key? Tell us, or we'll lynch you two as well!' There were loud shouts of concurrence.

Fear showed in Buller's boyish face. 'Marshall Colpett's got it. He took it home with him.'

'You're lyin'!' somebody called out, and immediately both deputies were frisked, and then the drawers in the desk and the hooks on the wall were searched but no key was forthcoming.

'OK,' Hardwright said, 'so we'll have to believe this young sprite. He turned to the man standing at his shoulder. 'Take Evans with you. Get the key from the marshal. His house is at the top end of the street. If he makes trouble drag him back here.'

The two men nodded and pushed their way through the others and out through the door.

Frank was panting. The air seemed suffocating. He counted eight vigilantes left in the office, including Hardwright.

'You're making a big mistake,' he called out. 'I'm not the rapist.'

Hardwright unleashed a scornful laugh. 'Lies won't save your soul. Confess what you did and the Devil may burn you a bit quicker!'

The comment brought jeers from the others, then a man from the back shouted, 'We don't need no key. Let's just shoot the bastard and be done with it!'

Hardwright quashed the suggestion by saying, 'We'll conduct this affair as true vigilantes; we'll have ourselves a fair lynchin'.'

Like scolded children, his men quieted to such an extent that Frank became aware of the tick of the wall clock.

He wished he'd heeded Rebecca's wishes to stay at home and not come on this crazy venture. He consoled himself that this was the only regret he would take to his grave. Mind you, he had plenty of sins to account for; he just prayed the Lord would be merciful.

Right then the two messengers returned, frogmarching the marshal at gunpoint. The lawman was still in his nightshirt with a jacket thrown over the top. He was incandescent with rage.

'What the hell are you playin' at, Hardwright? You got no right to burst in here. This man'll get a trial and if he's found guilty he'll face the consequences and — '

Hardwright cut across him. 'We're tired of your pussy-footin' law. Hand over the key and we'll get the lynchin' done.'

Support rippled around the room.

The marshal had no intention of complying. The two vigilantes had burst into his house and dragged him from his bed. For security he'd put the keys on a chain around his neck. He'd had no opportunity to remove them. Now his arms were seized and the key was found. A second later it was in the cell lock and turned.

But suddenly Marshal Colpett yelled out, 'Hold on! Hold on! Before you lynch this man, you should make damn sure he's who you think he is. There's only one person who saw the rapist and that's Jake Fox. He's the only one who can identify him.'

Somebody else said, 'Fox is outa town. He's away in Jefferson City.'

The mob was impatient to carry out the lynching; however, Hardwright regretted that Fox was not there to see vigilante justice being meted out. After all, he had promised the hostler that he'd catch the rapist.

But now he felt he had no option. He said, 'All right. Let's get the lynchin' over with.'

10

Jake Fox's intention to take his wife on to Jefferson City had been abruptly halted when a cowboy from Modoc Falls arrived at the relay station with the news that the one-armed rapist had been captured and was in the marshal's jail. White-hot malevolence was reignited in Jake. He imagined getting his hands around the man's throat, seeing his eyes bulge as he throttled the life from him.

In consequence, he now knew he must return to Modoc Falls. When the stage doing the return run from Jefferson City departed from the relay station, he and the tottering Margaret were aboard it. The prospect of going back home had revived her somewhat — so had the knowledge that the rapist was in custody. She had no wish to see him, but she knew that Jake would want to confront him, breathe into him his hatred, before the law took its course. She wondered if a court would pass down a death sentence. She regretted that it might not. The man, whilst responsible for Carolyn's death, hadn't actually murdered her — and rape might not be a capital offence. But she recalled how Hardwright had assured Jake that he would lynch the man. And she truly wished that would happen.

Now husband and wife were back in town. Jake had soon become aware that the vigilantes had stormed the jail. Such action could only mean one thing — a lynching. He knew, above all else, that he wanted to watch as the man who had raped his beloved Carolyn slowly choked to his death.

In consequence he hastily limped up the street towards the jail, hoping he wasn't too late to see the spectacle. He wished he'd glimpsed the rapist's face when he came to the livery that night. It would have made recognition so much easier.

Frank realized how futile any resistance on his part would be. He did not need strong-arm tactics from his persecutors to drag him from the cell, but stepped out calmly. He ignored the profane accusations that were showered upon him: 'You damned girl-molester! You filthy rapist!'

Meanwhile Jake Fox barged straight into the crowded marshal's office and immediately saw the man being dragged from the cell. His heart was pumping, his hatred overflowing.

'I hear you got the sonovabitch who raped my Carolyn. If you're gonna lynch him, I wanna see it!'

He would have preferred to kill this demon himself, although he knew that Hardwright would make a good job of it. However, there was one thing he could do. He elbowed his way forward to confront the condemned man.

Jake glared flush into his face. If his eyes could have spat venom right then, they would have done so. But he wasn't through. Bunching his fists, he struck Frank a thumping blow on the jaw.

Frank reeled back, but his jaw was unusually hard, and he drew himself upright again. 'I didn't rape your daughter!' he stated.

'Filthy liar!' Jake cursed him with a string of obscenities and cuss words.

Suddenly Frank wrenched his handless arm from the vigilante holding him. He waved the still-bandaged stump defiantly. He cried out so that all could hear, 'If you're intent on hanging an innocent man, let's get it over with!'

And then a strange thing happened. Dismay flooded Jake's face and his jaw dropped. Recollection came to his mind with surprising clarity. Frank's right hand was missing. He recalled that the rapist had lost his *left* hand. He'd noticed at the time that the man still had the use of his gun hand.

In that instant he knew that this man was not the brute he reviled.

As Frank was about to be marched

from the office to the street outside where a hang-rope dangled from a convenient branch, Jake screamed out, 'Stop! Hold on, for heaven's sake! You got the wrong man!'

Taken aback, the gathering shuffled to a halt.

'What the hell d'you mean?' Hardwright demanded. 'Don't you wanna see justice done?'

'I do.' Jake was breathing heavily, his face flushed. 'But this fella ain't guilty. You got the wrong man.'

'How d'you damn well know?'

Jake told them.

The mob lapsed into silence, utterly deflated. Jake looked at Frank and said, 'I'm right sorry, mister. Sorry you've had all this trouble. Sorry I hit you.'

Frank raised his hand to his face, which was turning red with the bruise.

Into the stunned hush, he spoke. 'I forgive you. I guess you just saved my life and for that I'm beholden.'

All the tension had left the gathering and men were shuffling away, moving into the street, mumbling their disgust at events.

Hardwright looked uncharacteristically contrite. He smoothed his great beard. In a quiet voice he said, 'I guess we better catch the real rapist, then.'

Soon the office had emptied apart from the marshal, his deputies and Frank.

Frank returned to his cell and collapsed on to the bunk. In all his varied experience he'd never come closer to his final moment. It would take him a long while to shake off the feeling that he was about to step into the next world. But he was convinced that the Lord had saved him — the Lord and Jake Fox.

★   ★   ★

Next morning he left the marshal's office. Colpett shook his hand and said, 'I'm real sorry about what happened.'

Frank stepped away with an acknowledging nod.

He reminded himself that he still had work to do. He walked to the livery and hired a lively, young mustang, black as night. Jake Fox wasn't in sight. Another man was standing in for him.

Before he left town, Frank filled his saddlebags with a good supply of provisions from the general store: salt pork and hard-tack.

He was still shaken, there was no denying that, but as he rode out, he tried to banish the shattering experience of the previous night from his mind.

What was the best course of action he could now take? He decided that he would return to the Lava Fields. It somehow seemed the focal point if he were to stand any chance of retrieving the situation. From there he might be able to track down the kidnapper. On the way, he would call at the Bramptons' place. There would be no welcome there, but he reasoned that maybe he could find some clue regarding the stolen ransom.

Two hours later, with the sun stoked up to blazing ferocity, the decrepit buildings of the Bramptons' farm came into sight. Frank reined in, dismounted and hitched the mustang to a gnarled stump. He knew he must be cautious, or he might be greeted with a bullet. If it was Hector Brampton who had followed him, and then stolen the ransom, he would be in no mood to extend hospitality. Not that he ever had been.

Frank approached slowly, using what scant cover there was. The wreck of the house shimmered in the heat. It looked utterly quiet, utterly deserted, but he wasn't taking any chances. He reached the crumbling boards of the veranda. Still no sign of life.

He paused, listening for a moment, his senses alert. Finally, he was convinced that nobody was at home. Perhaps the couple had absconded to enjoy the perceived fruits of the theft.

He tried the door. It was locked. He stepped to the side, gazed through the dust-coated window.

He grunted with shock. A body was sprawled faceup on the floor, a knife jutting from its chest. There was no mistaking the small form of Hector Brampton.

11

The suspicion came to Glassner's daughter, Lucille, like another nail in her coffin. She believed she was with child.

She was huddled in the depths of a huge cave, in a chamber lit only by the dying embers of a small fire. Smoke thickened the air. Above her, she knew, bats were hanging from the roof. She was bound hand and foot, as she had been for much of the two months of her captivity. Her entire body was wracked with pain, brought on by the cramped position she was forced to keep. She was filthy, for there was no water in which to wash. What clothes she'd been wearing at the time of her kidnap — jodhpurs and shirt — had been reduced to soiled rags.

Right now, she was alone.

While she guessed that outside the

sun was torrid, within the cave the temperature was a gloomy low. She shivered and tried to wriggle closer to the embers of the fire.

Soon after she'd been kidnapped, Victorio had joined his partner — the one-handed man, Harp Banderas. She hated and feared both of them, but Banderas was the worst. Whilst Victorio beat and threatened her, he did not molest her sexually. Banderas did. He had raped her many times, satisfying his lust, and destroying every vestige of her 18-year-old dignity and innocence. If ever it came within her power, she would gladly murder both of them.

She was sure Banderas's seed had taken root inside her, and if she survived, she would bear a monster, like him. She howled with despair.

They had been gone for a good hour, but she didn't know where to. They were angry because the ransom had not been delivered, and they had taken their frustration out on her with a beating. They had said that her father obviously did not want her back because he had not paid the money they had demanded. Victorio had complained that he was tired of her and would kill her soon unless the ransom was forthcoming. She wondered if death would be best, because life in captivity was an unrelenting nightmare. Since being incarcerated in the cave she had only been allowed outside each morning and evening for brief moments to attend to her toilet — and even that was at the end of a rope.

Yesterday she'd overheard Victorio and Banderas talking about the telegram sent to her father. Apparently Victorio, who was not a marked man in this region, had travelled to Jefferson City and despatched a message through Western Union. Being left alone with Harp Banderas for the three days he was gone had perhaps been the worst experience of Lucille's wretched captivity.

She wondered if her father had really decided he did not want her back. She felt that she had never known him very well. He was completely involved with his political activities and, in the years since her mother had died, he'd shown little interest in her. Although he'd never deprived her of money, nor any of the luxuries of life, revelations of love, of tenderness, were not part of his make-up. Above everything, he wanted to be President and his mind was completely focused on his aspirations. If, by some miracle, she survived this ordeal, she suspected that, once he knew that she was pregnant with a bastard child, he would disown her, banish her to some remote place. He would not tolerate the shame she brought, particularly so if he gained the presidency.

And perhaps Jim Esthelder, the man she had promised to marry, would no longer want her. Surely no man would have a woman so drastically soiled.

Victorio had made awesome threats that if she ever attempted escape, he would cut her hand off so she would be like Banderas. Banderas had smiled and relished the prospect and suggested that both hands would be better.

But now the two of them were away. The prospect of somehow escaping grew in her mind, and she devised a plan. Firstly she had to make sure her tormentors were not returning. She strained her ears, listening intently. She heard nothing apart from the stirrings of the bats above her.

Hoping, pleading, for good luck, she stretched out her legs. She dragged herself closer to the fire, manoeuvring her body until the embers began to singe the binding rope. Clenching her teeth, she suffered the scorching pain until the rope gave and her feet were free. Her hands were even more difficult; her wrists and arms became burned, but she persevered until her hands were free. She was flushed with sudden joy. She tried to stand up but her legs gave out and she fell back. On the third attempt she managed to stay upright. She hoped that movement would have strength return to her limbs. Now all she had to do was get to the mouth of the cave and escape into the Malpais, then strive to find some place far off where she could hide. Come night, she would travel on, to where she didn't know, but freedom beckoned her.

Imbued with a renewed determination, she was about to move forward, when her heart missed a beat. She heard the voices and approaching footsteps of Victorio and Banderas. Panic took hold of her.

She dropped back down, trying to assume her previous position, but it was hopeless. When they stepped into the chamber, Victorio realized immediately what she'd been doing; maybe he smelled the burnt rope. He unleashed a great snarl and sprang at her, grabbing her arm, beating her back and buttocks unmercifully with his hand. Harp Banderas stood back, his laughter mingling with her screams.

After a moment, he called out,

'Victorio, why don't you keep your promise? Cut her hands off, maybe her feet, too. That'll stop her escapin'!'

Breathless with the effort of doling out punishment, Victorio cast her aside like worthless trash.

Banderas said, 'Borrow my knife. It'll do the job fine. If you won't do it, I will!'

Still panting, Victorio nodded his great shaggy head. 'I might just do it.'

Lucille gazed at him like a trapped animal, her eyes wide with terror.

It was then that a great explosion occurred, its reverberating sound trapped within the confines that led to the chamber, blasting their ears into sudden deafness.

Both men had staggered.

As they recovered and their hearing returned, Victorio's voice came, hoarse with shock. 'What in tarnation was *that*!'

In the hours that followed, they came nowhere near to reasoning out the cause of the disturbance. Eventually, Victorio decided that it was the spirits bringing some message to him, maybe a warning from his Apache forebears. That night his reasoning was strengthened by the dream that came to him . . . a dream telling him that Frank Glengarry was in the Lava Fields hunting for him. And then he saw the vision of that same man, lying dead with blood upon him.

12

The telegram arrived at the Glassner ranch by special courier. During his political campaign the senator had made arrangements for all communications to be delivered with utmost urgency. His heart started beating faster as he realized this message came from a town he had never heard of in California. Since Glengarry had departed with the ransom he had heard nothing.

As he read the message, his spirits plunged.

Glassner,
You didn't get the money delivered like we told you. You got one more chance. Deliver money to same place two weeks from today. If you don't, your daughter dies. Also, if you try any tricks, we will kill her. And we will spread

rumours that before she died, she told us how you sexually abused her and how she was glad to get away from you. Remember, this is your last chance.

Wilber Glassner was sitting at the desk in his study. Now he buried his face in his hands and did something that he thought he would never do. He wept, his tears misting up the lenses of his spectacles. He feared that all his plans would come tumbling down. He shuddered with despair.

What in God's name had happened to Glengarry? Why hadn't he kept his word and done as arranged? Maybe he'd gone off, making the most of the fake money before the fraud was discovered. Maybe he'd taken up with some fancy woman, chucked his religious principles out of the window and disappeared into obscurity!

And what proof was there that Lucille was not already dead?

He hammered his fists on his desk

with frustration. Wasn't running for the presidency demanding enough without having the burden of knowing that if rumours were spread, his dreams would be over? His diary was fully booked. Within days he would embark on his nationwide tour, when he, as a man of utter integrity, would expound his visions of family values, of honest dealings, of decent behaviour. Now it could all come to nothing.

For a full five minutes he surrendered to deepest depression. Eventually, he hammered his fist on his desk. He straightened his back. He wiped his spectacles with his polka-dot handkerchief. Above all else, Wilber Glassner reminded himself, he was a fighter. He must not give in. If he could not succeed one way, he would have to use alternative means. Maybe he would have to meet the demands of the kidnapper or kidnappers, whoever they were. He didn't know why, but his plan to use forged money had backfired. It now seemed that he had no alternative but to meet the ultimatum of his persecutors, and pray that the affair remained out of the public eye.

His thoughts focused on Jim Esthelder.

His hand was trembling as he penned a note to the wheelwright, asking him to come to the ranch immediately. He had little regard for the man but he realized that such sentiments would have to be put aside. He would seek his help. He was confident that Esthelder's love for Lucille was sincere, and he would surely carry out any action that might bring about her release; namely, making a better job of delivering the ransom than Glengarry had.

Glassner left his study and gave the note to his foreman for delivery. After that he started to make immediate plans to raise the cash. This time it would have to be genuine.

*   *   *

Frank drew back from the window and stood on the rotting wood of the veranda, gathering his thoughts. The sight of the corpse of Brampton sprawled on the floor, blackened as it was with a seething fog of flies, had stunned him. He had no wish to enter the house. The stillness of the place convinced him that nobody else was there. He tried to fit together recent events. He had little doubt that it was one of the Bramptons who had robbed him of the ransom. It could have been either husband or wife; it was of little consequence which one it was right now. He could imagine that the two had quarrelled over the apparent fortune they'd obtained, quarrelled to such an extent that violence had broken out, and the woman, a strapping giant compared to her diminutive husband, had emerged the victor when she'd used the kitchen knife. Afterwards, she'd probably absconded with the loot, glad to be rid of the husband she hated, and anxious to enjoy her sudden wealth, completely ignorant of the fact that it was worthless.

Frank had three options open to him. The first was to chase after her, following what tracks he could find. He might then be able to recover the ransom and return in the hope of establishing contact with the kidnappers, handing over the haversack and thus gaining the release of Lucille.

Or, he could try and find a town in which the telegraph was operating. He could contact Glassner requesting further instructions.

The third option was to proceed directly to the Lava Fields. Thoughts of the girl, and the terrible plight she must be in, convinced him that this was what he must do. Too much time had already been wasted. He needed to find some clue as to where she was being held.

He knew it would be hopeless to take his horse further. The needle-sharp rocks would rip his hoofs to shreds. So he left the animal in the Bramptons' corral, ensuring that there was an ample supply of fodder. There was a water pump in the yard, and from this he obtained reluctant drips of water. He transferred what he could to the trough in the corral. It was slow work, but nonetheless he also managed to replenish his own canteen. Then he started out on foot, knowing that he had a hard-sweating slog ahead of him, the sun being a huge fireball that burned his back and neck.

★　★　★

He was downright weary when he reached Cullen's Ridge and looked over the Lava Fields.

They presented the usual, seemingly lifeless expanse of lava, reaching out towards the old Indian stronghold. To the east was the range of high volcanic mountains.

After a brief rest close to the cave where he'd spent the eventful night, he rose to his feet, determined to make the most of the remaining daylight. He reasoned that the area of the juniper tree would be the place to begin his search for Lucille. But first he had to traverse the treacherous expanse of intervening ground. It was here that the soldiers had come to grief in a hail of Indian bullets when they'd attempted to storm the stronghold fifteen years ago.

He progressed, stumbling and knowing that if he went down, he would lacerate himself on the razor-sharp rocks. Once, he did fall and rose with bloody hand and knees. It took him well over an hour to reach the juniper tree. On arrival, he gazed around, seeking anything that might provide evidence of the kidnapper, but there was nothing. A wave of doubt came over him. Was he wasting his time? He felt incredibly alone.

With night now descending, he could do no more.

The juniper tree was the landmark that indicated the entrance to the shadowy stronghold, which was, in fact, a crescent of rocks. He had read that the place was a maze of natural trenches and dugouts, and had dozens of connecting caves which were actually potholes formed when the lava boiled eons ago. If the kidnapper was here, and perhaps also the girl, he might never find them . . . unless they found him first.

He entered the stronghold by means of a path. He found a crevice in which he could find shelter; an owl flapped skywards from it as he entered, a mouse in its beak. He satisfied himself that no snakes lurked within the crevice, and settled down for the night. Presently, he slept.

He awoke as dawn's grey light was filtering in across the dreary landscape. He had slept the night through. His body ached with stiffness and pain. He rose, stretching the kinks from his arms and legs.

It was then that a great explosion rolled across the land, stronger than the loudest thunder. It was followed by more explosions, coming like a cannonade.

13

With half his fat fee, paid by local farmers, already in his pocket, William 'Cloudbuster' Ketchum, the rainmaker from Chicago, was concentrating on the task in hand. He knew that if he failed, he wouldn't get his fee. Also, Marshal Colpett would lose his job and be forced to face irate farmers. But Ketchum wasn't contemplating failure, not yet.

Ketchum had a pompous air. He wore a smart suit, a ribbon-tie and a stiff-brimmed hat. His neatly trimmed moustache and beard formed an almost perfect diamond on his face. He smoked a stogie continuously.

Originally he'd intended setting up his paraphernalia near town — rockets, kites, cannon and explosives — but the local women had been up in arms, claiming such activity would frighten the children and dogs. In consequence, coming via a circuitous route and passing a dried-up lake, he'd driven to the Lava Fields in his mule-drawn wagon, knowing that if he could make rain fall over this arid area, it would spread wide, bringing the desperately needed moisture to the surrounding land.

Over the past three days, he'd flown his kites into the clouds, each one bearing a slow-fused bomb, creating a bone-shaking blast, but no rain fell.

On the fourth day he decided it was time to load and prime his cannon. With his four-foot match he lit the fuse and created another ear-numbing explosion, then prepared a line of rockets, firing them off one by one. Finally, he set his biggest rocket for its highest trajectory. Using his giant match, he touched it off and it wobbled erratically heavenward. At the zenith of its flight it hung for a moment, then exploded in one tremendous salvo.

He watched anxiously for five minutes but no change came over the searing sky. With his ears still ringing, he was unaware at first of the approaching figure.

★   ★   ★

'Good morning to you, sir,' Frank greeted him. He was amazed to find another human being so close at hand. He had come to discover the cause of the booming explosions.

Ketchum started at his sudden presence but soon recovered his composure.

'May I ask you what you are doing?' Frank inquired.

'It's my pleasure to explain,' Ketchum nodded. 'I am striving to increase precipitation. You may have noticed the arid state of this territory caused by lack of rain. I am employed by the local farming community to remove or mitigate the drought by so-called cloud seeding. This is done by firing into the clouds a mixture of silver iodide and salt powder mixed with a high degree of expertise. In other words I am a weather modifier.'

Frank nodded and wondered if prayer would be more effective.

Ketchum said, 'Perhaps I might inquire what brings you to this godforsaken region.'

'I am looking for a girl,' Frank stated.

'Well, sir, I would imagine you'd get more luck at a bawdy house in town than out here.'

'The girl in question,' Frank said, irritated that this man should associate him with such establishments, 'has been kidnapped and is being held, I believe, somewhere in this area. I was supposed to have delivered the ransom but I was bitten by a snake and the ransom was stolen.'

The rainmaker raised a quizzical eyebrow. 'It is a good story. You are not the first sign of human life I have encountered here over the last few days.'

Frank's ears perked up. 'Who have you seen?'

Ketchum eyed him, as if debating whether or not to reveal his information. He decided in the affirmative. He took a draw on his stogie, then said, 'About half a mile from here, there's a whole group of ice caves, though I doubt they hold much ice in this arid season. Mighty large they are. I saw a one-handed man entering a cave.'

'When?'

'Oh, a couple of days ago, I guess.'

'Did he see you?' Frank asked.

'No. I made sure I kept hidden because he looked to be an unsavoury individual.'

Frank's mind was racing. This man could be the kidnapper as well as the rapist! 'He might be the one holding the girl. Could you take me to that cave?'

'I'll point the cave out to you,' Ketchum nodded. 'Maybe by the time I get back here, rain will be falling.' He smiled. 'This place seems overcrowded with one-handed men.'

Frank shrugged off the remark. He helped Ketchum load his equipment up on his canvas-topped wagon, then with the rainmaker leading the way, they started off, the ground rising beneath their feet. Twenty minutes later they were in higher terrain, the rock faces darkened with the gaping holes of cave entrances.

But now Ketchum showed uncertainty. On reflection he couldn't be sure which cave was the one in question. Eventually he indicated a particularly wide opening.

'I think,' he said, 'that's it.'

'I hope you're right,' Frank said. 'It'll be mighty dark inside.'

'No fear,' Ketchum remarked. 'I have matches.' He paused, pondered briefly and added, 'It seems to me that if that fella is holding the young lady captive, he may not welcome any intrusion.'

'You're right,' Frank affirmed. 'I don't aim to let him see me first.'

'Then I shall donate my matches to you,' Ketchum said grandly, 'wish you good fortune and wait here.'

'I appreciate your help.'

Doubts nagged at Frank. Ketchum wasn't sure he'd indicated the right cave.

Furthermore, Frank was assuming that 'One-Hand' was not only the rapist, but also the kidnapper of Lucille Glassner.

He had to make sure.

He drew his Colt, checked that it was fully charged and hoped he would not have to fire it. But if circumstances demanded it, he felt that God would not blame him for ridding the world of a wicked devil. Whatever happened, he must not place the girl in further jeopardy — if indeed she was present at all.

He clambered down a slight slope and walked forward, placing his feet so as to avoid dislodging stones. Ahead, sudden movement caught his eye. He tensed, gun raised, then relaxed. Only a lizard skittering across the lava.

The cave entrance loomed before

him like a yawning mouth. He paused, straining his ears for sound, but he heard nothing untoward. He stepped into the gloomy interior, aware that a coldness had replaced the outside heat. He saw how a passageway led off to one side. He crept into it. The roof sloped down so that he had to be careful not to bump his head.

The lingering doubt persisted. Was this the wrong cave? Was he on a fool's mission?

He emerged into an inner chamber and immediately noticed that a whiff of stale smoke hung on the air. There was practically no light now. He listened again, holding his breath, and finally he was convinced that there were no humans here. He struck one of Ketchum's matches on the sole of his boot and as his eyes adjusted to the sudden flare, he saw what was left of a rough camp — empty cans and rye bottles scattered about, an old discarded blanket and the spot where a fire had been. As the match scorched his fingers and spluttered out he concluded that 'One-Hand' and the girl, if she was with him, had vacated this hideaway.

He crouched down and felt the ashes. He drew his hand away quickly. They were still hot.

He felt excited. Hot ashes meant his quarry had only recently quit the cave.

★   ★   ★

For three days he hunted through the mountains, desperate for some clue. Ketchum was a good friend and sometimes accompanied him. With, as yet, no sign of rain, the rainmaker was reluctant to go back to town. They returned each night to the campsite that Ketchum had set up, discussing everything from religion to rainmaking. They watched the stars overhead and Ketchum marvelled at the wonders of the universe, but Frank could seldom relax. He was so haunted by the frustrations of his mission.

Each day they had searched caves, ravines, ancient bare lava shelves and other possible campsites but had found no evidence. Eventually Frank had to admit to himself that the kidnapper and the girl, if she still survived, could be miles away by now. In utter desperation he, once again, considered returning to Modoc Falls. If the telegraph lines were restored, he could send a message to Glassner explaining what had happened. He wished he could have informed the senator, and indeed Rebecca, of events earlier but he'd had no opportunity.

But when the rainmaker left, intent on going back to town, Frank decided not to accompany him. He asked Ketchum to call in at the Brampton place and take his horse back to town.

14

Jim Esthelder arrived at the Bramptons' farm, weary from his long
journey to California, carrying the
bulky haversack. But excitement was
growing in him. He might soon achieve
the release of the girl he yearned to
marry. Right now he needed respite for
himself and his horse; otherwise he
would not have stopped at this place.
He gazed at the farmhouse. It looked
as though a strong gust of wind would
have it tumbling down. He stepped on
to the decrepit planks of the veranda
and hammered on the door. He
waited, tried again but got no
response; the emptiness just echoed
back at him. Out of curiosity, he
moved along the veranda and peered
through the window. At first he
thought the mound on the kitchen
floor was a mountain of seething flies.

The window was open at the top, and suddenly the most foul stench wafted to his nostrils. He gagged and knew that it came from a rotting corpse. He stumbled back and at that moment heard the creak and rattle of an approaching wagon.

He was just returning to the yard as the rainmaker, puffing on his stogie, brought his mules to a halt. They needed no second invitation for they had been hobbling, their hoofs chipped and bleeding, and foam was caked around their mouths.

Brief introductions over, Jim imparted his alarming news. A peep through the window and a sniff of the foul air assured the rainmaker of something Glengarry had already told him.

Ketchum said, 'I'll let the marshal know about this as soon as I get back to town, that's if these damn mules make it. Tell me, what brings you to these godforsaken parts?'

Jim gave him a few details and

Ketchum showed surprise.

'You're the second fella with the same story — '

'What was his name?' Jim interrupted.

'Can't rightly remember . . .' Ketchum pondered, then he said, 'Oh yes, it was Glengarry. Claimed he'd been bitten by a snake and had the ransom money stolen.'

Jim grunted, astounded. 'Where is he now?'

'Last I saw of him, he was carrying on his search for that girl.'

A look of urgency came over Jim. 'I've got to get goin',' he said. 'With all those sharp rocks, I'll have to leave my horse here. I've got a long walk ahead of me.'

'You certainly have, young man. I wish you good luck and hope you find that poor girl.'

Ketchum remembered Frank's horse and he fastened it to the rear of the wagon. Then the two men shook hands and went their separate ways.

*　*　*

Victorio and Harp Banderas had made their temporary campsite at the side of a gulley. Both men were aware that the hour was approaching for the delivery of the ransom. This time, they hoped, there would be no hitch. Victorio had spent twenty minutes, passing the rope around a large boulder before fastening it to the girl's feet and wrists. The boulder had been convenient, but it had one drawback. It was positioned at the bottom of the gulley, which, if flooded, would prove a death trap for the girl. But Victorio didn't care about that. She would soon be surplus to his plans.

Lucille remained completely passive, resisting nothing, all her spirit long departed.

Now Victorio was preparing for the walk through the stronghold to the juniper tree. 'You stay here with the girl,' he told Banderas. 'I'll come back with the money, then we can share it out.'

'How do I know you'll come back?' Banderas asked.

'You have my word,' Victorio grinned wolfishly.

Banderas didn't believe him.

* * *

Meanwhile, Jim Esthelder was nigh exhausted after his long walk and final journey across the awesome rocks of the Lava Fields to the juniper tree, all the while clutching the bulky haversack. Now he rested it down and gazed around at the forlorn landscape. He had made it to the demanded place where the ransom was to be handed over and, he prayed, Lucille released. Excitement was growing in him at the prospect of seeing her again, of taking her in his arms, but then he began to wonder what difference these weeks of captivity had made to her. Had she been ill-treated, frightened . . . abused? He shuddered at the thought. If she had, he'd gladly kill her tormentor. He tried to rein in his emotions.

He checked his pocket watch. It was about an hour before the appointed time for the exchange. He sat on a rock and gazed around. He'd never experienced such a lonely and desolate place. The only sign of life came from the lizards darting across the rocks. And high in the sky, a buzzard.

The hour dragged by and there was no sign of the kidnapper. He wondered if whoever it was would fail to turn up. Had he travelled all this way for nothing? And what had become of Glengarry? Numerous questions pounded at him as the minutes passed.

Then, at last, he heard the rattle of a stone disturbed by somebody's foot and he turned to see a large, swarthy figure emerging from the stronghold, looking like a black crow.

Victorio raised his hand in greeting, a grin on his bearded face. 'Where is Glengarry?' he said.

'You have Lucille?' Jim asked. 'You will release her?'

'All in good time. Let me see the ransom first.'

Jim gestured towards the haversack and, without turning his back, Victorio went to it, unfastened its straps and looked inside. He grunted with satisfaction as he saw the wads of banknotes. He refastened the bag and hoisted it on to his shoulder.

'And now,' Jim said, 'you will release Lucille. You have her close by?'

'She is not here,' Victorio said. 'She is sick.'

Jim growled with displeasure, sensing a double-cross. 'It was part of the agreement.'

Victorio spat contemptuously. 'And what,' he snarled, 'are you gonna do about it?'

It occurred to Jim that Lucille might already be dead. Anger erupted in him and he stepped forward, attempting to rip his gun from its holster. But he was a wheelwright, not a gunman like his adversary. Victorio's hand was a blur as he snatched his own Colt. It was belching flame before Jim's weapon cleared its leather. The bullet struck the younger man in the chest, throwing him back and down. When he hit the ground, he lay unmoving, a bloody patch staining his shirt front.

Victorio re-holstered his gun and gave the body a cursory glance, prodding it with his boot. He grunted with satisfaction.

Presently, the buzzard sensed blood from its lofty vantage point and circled lower. It wasn't long before it had landed alongside the body.

★　★　★

Some inner instinct convinced Frank to remain in the area for a day or so more. He determined to return to his original campsite on Cullen's Ridge. He took a circular route through up-juts of lava and had almost reached the ridge when he heard the distant crack of a gun. The detonation seemed to hang on the still air. For a moment he couldn't be certain where the sound had come from, then he spotted the rapidly descending buzzard. It landed close to the distant juniper tree. He focused his field-glasses on the spot, but it was too far away to make detail out. The buzzard stayed down and shortly more scavengers arrived and landed close to the first bird.

He decided he must investigate and set out across the Lava Fields, cutting his boots in his haste. Soon his pace slowed, but he struggled on. With the tree growing closer, he saw something red amid the scrabbling birds. At his approach, they flapped a short distance away and watched him indignantly.

At first he did not recognize the corpse, but gradually recognition dawned on him and he spoke the name, 'Jim Esthelder'. He'd only met him once but he recalled the blue-eyed, handsome and powerful-looking young man he'd met at the wheelwright's in Travis Springs. Esthelder, the ardent lover of

Lucille, had made a profound impression upon him.

He saw the bullet wound to the chest had oozed blood, soaking his shirt. He must have died instantly.

There was little he could do for Esthelder now, except drag him into a crevice and place rocks on top of the body. He worked manfully, blood staining his hand and his bandaged stump, and eventually he knew he had done his best to keep the buzzards off.

A moment of intense grief came over him. Here was a young couple who'd had so much future happiness to look forward to. Now all happiness had been stubbed out and his suspicions and his bitterness centred on the one-handed rapist.

He mouthed a prayer for the boy's soul, and another that he would somehow be able to put an end to his evil killer.

★   ★   ★

At the highest point in the stronghold, Victorio paused. This was where he had left his Sharps rifle, as he'd preferred to use his handgun for disposing of the messenger. From here, he had a good view over the Lava Fields. He dropped the haversack and opened it up. He had a desperate urge to check the money, to make certain he was not being swindled in any way. As he thumbed through the banknotes, his gratification grew to a feeling of ecstasy. He was now richer than he'd ever been in his life — not bad for a humble Apache warrior who had ridden with Cochise. But he begrudged the prospect of sharing the money with 'One-Hand' Banderas. He didn't trust the man, anyway. Victorio reminded himself that he no longer had any need for either him or the girl. His plans had borne fruit. He could head north to Canada where he'd be safe from the law, and he could enjoy everything for which he'd schemed.

But of one thing he was sure. If he doubled-crossed Banderas, he would hound him wherever he went. It would be necessary to dispose of the one-handed man.

There was also another matter to which he needed to attend. He had no idea why Glengarry had not shown up, but he still harboured a hope that the man was in this area.

He little guessed that this hope would be realized so soon.

Satisfied that the ransom had been fully paid, he replaced it in the haversack, which he fastened and was about to hoist on to his back when his glance happened to swing across the sprawling expanse of the Lava Fields. He tensed as he saw the lone figure approaching the juniper tree. He picked up his Sharps, sensing that he could not afford to have anybody finding the messenger's body before he'd had time to disappear from the immediate locality.

He lay, belly down, gazing through the sights, and waited for the intruder to reach the corpse. He watched him drag it into the adjacent rocks. He was now well within range. Victorio steadied himself; killing was becoming a habit that he enjoyed. He steadied his aim, his finger tightened on the trigger and the gun blasted off.

He saw his target thrown back on to the ground, lying motionless. *More fodder for the damn buzzards*, he thought.

15

After she'd plunged the kitchen knife into Hector's puny chest, Blanche had moved with haste. She harnessed their horse on to the wagon and rejoiced in the misguided belief that she had a fortune in the haversack. There was enough money, she thought, for her to travel to the ends of the earth if she chose; to escape to some place so distant and obscure that nobody would ever pin a charge of murder on her. She still congratulated herself on the way she had acquired the wealth, remaining unseen as she followed Glengarry, and then, while he was asleep, removing the haversack. Her delight had known no bounds when she discovered its contents. Of course Hector had shown a joy she had never seen in him before, saying they could split the loot two ways, then part company. She had resented his suggestion, saying she had acquired the money herself and she would not share it. He'd had the stupidity to fly into a temper. He'd even tried to punch her. She'd never seen him show such passion. But she could overwhelm him any day. By the time she'd reduced him to a quivering jelly, it was her turn to show anger. At that moment all the old resentment flared inside her. How she hated this weakling of a man! She'd grabbed the kitchen knife and was surprised how easily it slipped between his ribs and pierced what she assumed was his heart. He'd writhed in agony, coughed up blood and then expired.

On the third night after the murder, she'd halted the wagon in a small clearing in the woods. By now her original euphoria had cooled some-what, and she began to view things differently. She realized that she'd been foolish not to hide Hector's body before she'd left. Had she done that, nobody would have ever suspected that murder had taken place. They would merely have supposed that the couple had packed their bags and moved away. After all, there seemed nothing to keep them in that hovel of a place.

As she settled down in the wagon for the night she concluded that she might still have time to put matters right. Visitors to the farmhouse had been a rarity, although Glengarry might return for his horse. But with luck she would get back before he showed up. She still wondered why he hadn't succumbed to the drug. She'd taken little notice of Hector dropping off, for he'd always been a dozy fool. She would go back and hide Hector's corpse in some obscure spot, and then she would have no fear of pursuit by the law. But she would not take the haversack of money with her. There was always the possibility of being waylaid or even robbed. She would bury it, making sure she would be able to locate the place when she returned. Satisfied with her reasoning, she lapsed into sleep and dreamed of the man Glengarry and of how handsome he was. And how good it would have been if he'd accepted her offer. Damn him!

She was up early. She found a suitable spot beneath an aspen tree, scooped out a hole with a stick, and buried the haversack. Dawn's light was very weak and she noted how low the clouds were. She gazed around, attempting to imprint upon her mind the exact location.

Soon, she was on her way back.

*　*　*

The journey was wearisome; the old horse could manage nothing more than a tired plod. This time she did not stop at a guest house, as she had done on the way out.

Three days later, she allowed the animal to halt as she neared the farmhouse. The light was poor.

A darkness had now descended that was deeper than dusk. Suddenly that darkness became illuminated with frightening intensity as lightning forked the sky and thunder cracked out so loudly that the horse reared with panic, almost overturning the wagon. As she struggled to calm the animal, heavy rain fell, soaking her. It was the end of the drought.

When she stepped down on to the sodden ground, she was glad that everything seemed deserted and quiet, apart from the roar of the rain and the frantic neighing of a horse in the corral. She guessed it was the animal that Glengarry had left. It was, in fact, Esthelder's horse, but she didn't know that. Now it was desperate for freedom. In order to quiet it, she walked through the mud, opened the corral gate and allowed it to escape to find sustenance where it could.

Utterly bedraggled, she sloshed her way to the house. On opening the door she was assailed by the foul odour of death and the buzzing of flies. It seemed that no one had disturbed the body. True enough, when she entered the kitchen, she found Hector, or what remained of him after the flies had feasted. He was in the same position in which she had left him. Placing a scarf across her face, and carrying a blanket, she approached him, driving away the voracious insects and noting with distaste how maggots were squirming around the wound in his chest. She pulled out the knife, knowing that she must hide it. She placed a blanket over the body and wrapped it around. She then gathered Hector up and took him out into the rain. He seemed almost weightless. She could carry him beneath one arm.

She splashed through puddles as she crossed the yard to the barn where she found a spade. A further walk and she was in the field where Hector had planted his fruitless soya. All that remained now were useless, dried-out stems. The rain had come far too late. It would be fitting to bury Hector at this place of his great failure.

She set to work with the spade; she was a dismal, bedraggled figure. The earth was hard but she was strong, with wide shoulders and muscular arms, and she sweated despite the rain until she had a hole so deep that she was confident that its contents would remain undiscovered for eternity. Not even the wolves would dig that deep. She now had to drop the body into the grave before it filled with water. She recovered the blanket, considering she would have greater need of the item than her husband. Next, she gathered Hector up in her arms. But at that moment she froze.

A man's voice had called above the pound of the rain. 'Hi there!'

She straightened up, her heart pounding like a triphammer. She cursed blasphemously. She had been so preoccupied with her digging that she had completely missed seeing the group of riders. Now they approached, all hunched in their yellow slickers. There were ten men in the posse. At their head, she recognized the marshal, Harry Colpett, and riding at his side was the tall figure of vigilante chief Ben Hardwright. Surprisingly, they had set their differences aside and set up a partnership — lawmen and vigilantes. Their belief was that together they'd have a better chance of wiping out banditry in the region. Colpett also saw it as a means of preventing any repeat of the storming of the jail. They had ridden out soon after the rainmaker had arrived with the news.

Now they reined in their animals close to where the bedraggled woman was standing with her dead husband in her arms. She was about to drop him into his grave.

Colpett saw tears welling in her eyes, joining with the raindrops. He took it as an expression of grief. It was not. It was chagrin.

'Jesus!' the marshal cried out. 'What's happened?'

She burst into great sobs and her lips were unable to form words. But inwardly her brain was working frantically.

Colpett dismounted and rushed to her, putting a comforting arm around her shoulder.

'Help me,' she at last managed. 'Help me put my darling husband into his grave.'

As the others slipped from their saddles, there was no lack of helping hands. Hector Brampton was lowered into the soggy depths. A vigilante took up the spade and started to fill the grave in.

'My dear Mrs Brampton,' the marshal said, 'how did he die? What happened?'

She steeled herself for what she was about to relate. She had to be convincing.

'He was murdered,' she sobbed, 'killed in cold blood.'

'But why . . . and by whom?'

'This man came to the farm,' she went on. 'We gave him food, but afterwards he tried to kiss me. He

. . . he touched me . . . all in front of my dear husband. Then he grew wild and before I knew, he had me on the floor with my dress up around my ears and he was raping me.'

A wave of fury swept through the listeners.

'My husband went crazy,' she continued. 'He was so brave. He flew at the man, dragged him off me. There was a terrible struggle. And then the man grabbed a big knife from the table and he . . . he . . . ' She trailed off into another sob. After a moment she seemed to pull herself together. 'After he'd murdered Hector, he ran out. The last I saw of him he was heading towards the Lava Fields.' She lowered her face into her hands and howled. Presently she whispered, 'My dear, brave Hector. I loved him so much.'

There was more than one tear in the eyes of the men watching.

'When did this happen?' Colpett asked.

She hesitated, then said, 'Y-yesterday.

No, not yesterday. The day before. Tuesday.'

Hardwright was standing close by. His face was as dark as the sky. 'My God, we'll catch the bastard and lynch him to the nearest tree. We'll give him such a slow choke, he'll wish he'd never been born.'

Colpett asked, 'D'you know the man? D'you know his name?'

'Sure I do,' she said with bitterness in her voice. 'He's only got one hand. His name's Frank Glengarry!'

16

After Senator Wilber Glassner's rousing speech at the party convention, his nomination as presidential candidate had been a mere formality. Since then his campaign had gone from strength to strength, his popularity boosted by his splendid oratory. His bull neck and strong chin gave the impression of a man with unappeasable determination, the strong leader for whom the nation was crying out.

Now he was on his final whistle-stop tour. It was taking in vast expanses of the country, making appearances in such wide-flung states as Alabama, Missouri, Ohio and Michigan, and finishing up in Washington. Speaking from the rear platform of his hired train, he would make many inspiring speeches. Getting America back on its feet and recovering from its economic malaise were major themes, as were his intentions to create a stronger middle class. At every stop his popularity increased.

Only when he was alone at night in his luxurious train compartment, did his thoughts turn to the dark business of the kidnap. He wondered if Esthelder had delivered the ransom and Lucille was free. On the other hand, if anything had gone wrong, as it had done with Glengarry, his reputation could tumble like a house of cards, particularly if rumours of abuse were spread. But he tried to push such possibilities out of his mind and bask in the acclamation he was currently enjoying. And pray that the press did not seize upon the affair and make a scandal of it.

★   ★   ★

At his ranch in Texas, work continued under the supervision of the foreman, Tex Clayton; beeves were being gathered for the fall round-up.

In the fine ranch house things were quiet. The housekeeper, a half-Navajo woman called Elvita, was glad Glassner was away. She detested him, finding him a bully, who always complained about her work. But the pay was good.

One day, when she was dusting in the study, her eyes fell upon the drawer in his desk. Being of an inquisitive nature, she opened it and saw the folded telegram inside. She extracted it and gasped at what she read. It was a message to Glassner about his daughter . . . *before she died, she told us how you sexually abused her and how she was glad to get away from you.*

Elvita glanced around to ensure that she was not overlooked, then she slipped the telegram into the pocket of her apron.

That evening, at her home in Modoc Falls, she showed it to her husband.

'Take it to the newspaper office,' he advised her. 'They may pay good money for it.'

156

She nodded her dark head. She would do it in the morning. She would gladly destroy the dreams of her employer. The man she despised.

★ ★ ★

'Mrs Brampton,' the tall Hardwright had said as the posse prepared to leave the farm, 'you can rest assured we'll catch Glengarry and give him all the justice he deserves.'

Blanche had mumbled her gratitude and said, 'You're good men.' By now she was playing the grieving widow convincingly.

Marshal Colpett suggested that they could provide a man to escort her to town, to get away from this place where murder had occurred. Maybe she could take lodgings at the hotel.

'No,' she said, 'I would prefer to stay here, close to Hector's grave. I guess he'd feel awful lonely if I were to leave him.'

The men of the posse nodded their

understanding, seeing her as a courageous woman who had undergone terrible suffering. A person of true grit.

So they'd left her, riding out towards the Lava Fields. When the going became treacherous under hoof, they'd dismounted, left their horses in the care of one man, and proceeded on foot. They were determined to find Glengarry.

★   ★   ★

In truth, Blanche was desperate to get away from the farm. She quickly changed into dry clothing. She found Hector's slicker and put it on. It was far too small, but it was the best she had. Despite the long days of drought, she was now sick of the rain. With her horse rested, she climbed on to the wagon and set out, the prospect of recovering the haversack of cash filling her with hope of a new life, where the dismal past would be left behind.

Weary, rain-filled days later, she had

reached what she thought was the area where she had hidden the loot. She gazed around for the aspen tree, but everywhere seemed different; yet she was sure this was the place in which she'd spent that night. Leaving the wagon, she stumbled about for hours, splashing through puddles, wandering wide through forest. Still she could not locate the spot. At last she collapsed into the mud and wept tears of chagrin. Surely that damned aspen hadn't been washed away!

Eventually she scrambled up. Maybe she'd made a mistake, maybe she should search further on. Suddenly renewed misery struck her. She had roamed far from where she'd left the wagon. At the time she had not taken great notice; she'd been so excited by the prospect of recovering the money.

For a long while she plodded on in the downpour, moving through the woods in widening circles. Just when she should have been so happy, everything had gone hopelessly sour.

Lucille Glassner was shivering. She was certain she was very close to death and she was beyond caring. Her arms and legs were completely numb; they had been bound so often. The rest of her body was racked with pain, sodden and cold. She had given up struggling against the ropes.

The rain was beating down, feeling leaden as it struck her, and water gushed about her, flowing through the gulley with awesome power. The ropes binding her had grown tighter with the wetness, cutting off her circulation, and now the level of water in the gulley was rising. When it covered her face she'd decided she would submit and make no effort to survive.

★ ★ ★

In his lofty position in the stronghold, Victorio rose to his feet, lowering his rifle. Suddenly, the dream came to his mind, the dream that had told him that Frank Glengarry had been loitering in the area, intent on hunting him down. The dream had also told him that he would kill Glengarry. Now he sensed that his dream had been a true vision, a message from the spirits. The man he had shot could be none other than Glengarry. He considered walking to the body, making sure that there remained no sign of life. But then, with the rain pelting down and with the haversack growing more sodden by the minute, he changed his mind. From this distance, he studied the felled man, assuring himself that Glengarry was a corpse. The vision had been fulfilled. Now, perhaps, escaping with the money was the most important thing. Or so Victorio reasoned.

★   ★   ★

For what seemed an age, Frank lay upon the rocks, stunned. The sheer impact of being shot with a heavy-calibre bullet, albeit in the arm, had caused him to fall back. As his senses cleared, he felt the rain driving down upon him, and he realized that he was, more than ever, an easy target for the hidden marksman. He figured that his best chance for survival was to act as if he were dead, thus giving the impression that the use of further lead would be wasteful. Even so, being sprawled on his back, utterly helpless, half drowned, was not a reassuring position. And now there was more pain in his much-punished arm. The bullet had caught him just above the snakebite, slicing through the bandage that Doctor Briggs had applied and gouging out a chunk of flesh.

He feared that his attacker might approach him with no pleasant intent, but as the minutes passed he began to hope he was safe, at least for the present. Eventually, he decided to chance his luck. After weeks of drought, he was amazed that rain was falling. It was causing rivulets to run between the rocks. Had Ketchum really worked his magic?

He sat up, glanced around. Everywhere was mockingly dreary. All around him, the landscape was dismal. Gingerly, he climbed to his feet. He examined his arm. Doctor Briggs's bandage was now a tattered rag and was red with blood. In time, he suspected, loss of blood would weaken him to such an extent that he would collapse. But before that he wanted to find his enemy. He wanted that really badly. He gritted his teeth and started forward, wondering if his would-be killer was still somewhere close in the stronghold.

★   ★   ★

Harp Banderas wasn't sure whether the girl was alive or dead. She'd annoyed him by crying out and he'd put his hand around her throat, his thumb pressed deeply.

Afterwards, suspecting treachery, he had followed Victorio at a fair distance. He had heard the two shots, one from a handgun, the other from a rifle, the detonations just audible above the sound of rain on the rocks. He had waited patiently, hidden at the edge of the stronghold, confident that his erstwhile partner would return this way, hopefully bearing the loot. He was not disappointed.

Firstly, he heard Victorio's grunting breath. Moments later he appeared, following the path around the rock face, the haversack across his shoulder, his rifle in his hand. Banderas's temples were pounding. He needed to confront the man, make him realize 'One-Hand' Banderas couldn't be double-crossed. With his gun drawn, he leapt from his cover, blocking the way, his mocking laugh coming as a snarl.

For a second their eyes met. The glowering hatred they felt for each other had been suppressed only by their mutual greed to get the ransom. Now that hatred erupted. Banderas's finger tightened on his trigger. Sensing what was coming, Victorio threw himself to the side. Holding his rifle like a pistol, he also fired. Both men felt the bite of lead.

The heavy-calibre bullet, fired at close range, had blasted through Banderas's rib-cage, causing a gaping hole. He was thrown back in a mist of blood, dead before he hit the ground. Victorio remained on his feet, swaying. Banderas's shot had thudded into his thigh, angering him.

Victorio limped onward, clutching the haversack with one hand while his other was held against his wound, but his fingers soon became slippery with blood. He knew the lead was buried in his thigh. He stopped and sat down. *Damn Banderas!* he thought.

When he felt better he'd go back to the gulley where there were some rags he could use as a bandage. But for the moment he needed to rest his leg.

* * *

Frank had been within the stronghold when he heard the blast of gunfire, unmistakable despite the rumbling thunder. Suddenly he was scrambling desperately along the rocks. The whole place was a labyrinth of paths, caves and shadowy crevices. It was riddled with the paths the Indians had created years earlier. Twice he tripped on craggy rocks, ripping the knee of his denims and falling jarringly. But he struggled up, his instinct driving him towards the source of the shots, while he prayed that his strength would not drain away.

17

James Pollinger, owner of the *Travis Springs Gazette*, strongly supported Senator Glassner for President in his editorial columns. Now he picked up the envelope, personally addressed to him, and slit it open. He took out the telegram. When he asked around, he discovered that it had been brought in by the senator's housekeeper.

He immediately dismissed the slur of sexual abuse. He knew Wilber Glassner as a good, upright friend, and a superb candidate for the presidency. He placed the telegram in his drawer. He would give it to Wilber when he next came to his ranch. The housekeeper had asked for a reward for what she'd done. Pollinger smiled. She wouldn't get a cent! It would be up to Glassner whether or not he dismissed her.

★ ★ ★

Suddenly, when Blanche was about to collapse once more in total despair, she glimpsed the wagon ahead of her, the horse waiting patiently, and she cried out with relief.

She hauled herself up on to the seat and urged the animal into a motion. It was fifteen minutes later that she realized she'd made a stupid mistake. The aspen tree hadn't been washed away; it shone like a beacon before her.

Within seconds she was scrabbling at its base, crying out with joy as her fingers clawed into the earth. She pulled out the haversack. It was damp and dirty, but she didn't care. Soon the future would open up for her and she would experience the paradise she had dreamed of. At least, that is what she imagined.

A week of travel followed and then she reached Winnemucca, a fledgling settlement on the Central Pacific

Railroad. She booked into the Winnemucca Hotel, taking the finest suite. Here, she luxuriated in a hot, foamy bath.

In the days that followed, she spent extravagantly, buying the most elegant clothes on offer, and also some rare perfume; she enjoyed fancy cakes, rich coffee and lavish Basque meals in the best restaurant in town. In her new dresses and shaded by her parasol, she strolled through Pioneer Park, enjoying the scent of flowers. She attracted glances wherever she went. And all the while she pondered on what her next move should be, believing that the world was her oyster.

She realized that she couldn't keep the sackful of cash locked in her hotel room for much longer, so she extracted enough notes to meet her immediate needs and visited the First National Bank to deposit the bulk of it.

The teller raised his eyebrows at the sight of the wads of large-denomination notes.

'Would you wait for a minute, madam?' he said. 'I need to speak to the manager.'

She frowned with irritation.

Ten minutes later, both teller and manager returned and informed her that the money was fraudulent and that the police would be notified.

'Can't be fraudulent!' she gasped in horror, but they insisted.

A fit of dizziness came over her. She swayed on her feet, would have fallen had not a fellow customer struggled manfully to support her large body.

When she recovered, she left the bank, showing no gratitude to her saviour.

★　★　★

Frank would never know whether it was sheer good fortune or divine guidance that brought him to what he sought. He suspected the latter.

The continued haemorrhaging from his arm had weakened him as he stumbled to the rim of the gulley. For a moment all he could see was the powerful rush of water funnelling downwards. Then his gaze seized on to what at first appeared to be a bundle of rags bobbing on the surface. A dreadful vision came to him. Was he hallucinating?

But no.

After all his searching, *this!* The girl, lying facedown in the torrent, which, strangely, did not draw her along with it. Desperation somehow revitalized him and he slid down the gulley side and was soon thigh-deep in water. Fighting the current, he waded to the girl and scooped her head from beneath the surface. He realized that her body was restrained by a rope that encircled a large boulder. Supporting her head with his knee, he drew his pocketknife and hacked at the rope until it was sliced through.

A dismal feeling came over him that the girl was dead. She seemed nothing more than the limpest of rag dolls.

Gathering all the strength he could muster, using his hand and stump, he dragged her to the shale bank of the gulley and rested her down. He gazed into her blue-tinged face; her eyes were closed and he saw no sign of life. He turned her on to her side, probed his finger into her mouth and flicked out mucus. He lay beside her and pressed his lips to hers, forcing his breath into her, acting like bellows. On and on he persisted, inwardly praying that there was some spark of life left within her. After a while he alternated his breathing and applied pressure, with his hand, on her chest below her breasts.

And then it happened! All at once she coughed and vomited a stream of frothy pink fluid. Overjoyed, he doubled his efforts, careful not to break her ribs, working hard on her chest, and now he was feeling a reaction. As for himself, he had somehow forgotten his weakness and pain.

Ten minutes later, she was sitting up, although immense shudders enveloped her. She had coughed and vomited several times, but now her eyes were open and as she looked at him, her words were scarcely audible: 'You should've let me die . . . '

'No,' he cried fiercely. 'You must live. I will take you back home.'

He gazed at her but saw no comprehension in her face. He realized that her feet and hands were still bound. He hacked through the ropes, freeing her, seeing the blueness of her skin. She was so frail, he feared he might cause her further injury, but he was as gentle as he could be. Her teeth were chattering and her body was trembling. He did then the only thing he could think of. He took her in his arms and hugged her to him, hoping that some warmth from his own body would seep into her. He wished she'd speak, but she didn't, and he had the feeling that she had no wish to live.

The rain was easing off, and the light was fading fast. He reckoned his arm was no longer bleeding. He'd been lucky that the bullet had done only superficial damage before it passed on its way.

He tried to reason what further action he could take, but his mind came up with nothing. All he could do was survive for the moment, and provide what help he could, to comfort this girl, despite their bedraggled state. He prayed: *Please God, don't let her die.* Later, as the bleak night deepened, he sang Hanna hymns to her, but he didn't know whether she heard them or not.

★ ★ ★

'Don't move,' Victorio snarled. 'I know who you are, Frank Glengarry.'

He was standing higher up the bank of the gulley. Although he was hobbling with his wounded leg, he was no less menacing. His ugly, chunky features were distorted, the deep, knife-slash scar across his right cheek showing red; his dark eyes deep-set, predatory, and blazing malevolence.

Frank was crouching at the water's edge, washing the blood from his arm. He straightened up, dismay crushing him. He thought he'd been rid of Victorio; he'd been wrong.

'I will enjoy killin' you, real slow,' Victorio went on. 'I want you to suffer after what you did.'

'What did I do?' Frank demanded.

'You killed my brother, shot him through the heart.'

'Your brother?'

'Sure you did. You might remember the name ... Zackary 'Child-eater' Hawkes. He was my twin brother, my own flesh and blood.'

'I remember him all right,' Frank said, recalling his days as a Pinkerton detective. 'He would've killed me, if I hadn't got him first.'

'Well, if he was tryin' to kill you, I'll finish the job for him!'

Victorio laughed triumphantly, then pointed his gun at Frank. He paused for what seemed an eternity, then pressed the trigger, but the weapon misfired harmlessly.

On impulse, Frank moved with all the speed his jaded body could muster, leaping up the bank, yanking his own Colt from its holster. But Victorio grabbed his wrist, squeezed, and forced him to drop his weapon. Frank rammed hard into his opponent's groin with his knee; Victorio twisted. The two men were grossly mismatched. Victorio was ten years younger, stronger, and his great hulk loomed over Frank. He also had two hands. However, they each had wounds to contend with.

As they struggled, Frank realized that he wasn't going to get the better of this man physically.

He fought bravely, but gradually his stronger opponent overpowered him, hooking his leg behind his, causing him to fall back and down. With a howl of triumph, Victorio dropped his weight on top, crushing the breath from Frank. His hands came up and he grabbed

Frank around the throat.

'Now, my friend,' Victorio panted, his crazed face inches from Frank's, 'you'll die a slow, chokin' death, and even if my brother is in hell, he'll laugh and know you got what you deserved!'

Frank tried to break free, but it was hopeless. With his windpipe squeezed, his senses began to wane. He fought hard for breath but he was being choked in Victorio's iron grip.

Neither man had seen Lucille snatch up Frank's fallen gun. Without hesitation, she pressed the muzzle against Victorio's head and pressed the trigger. The blast was deafening. Victorio's skull burst open, ejecting a spurt of blood and brain.

With the strangling hold on his throat relaxed, Frank gulped in gunsmoke-tainted air; he waited a long minute and then, with what diminished strength he had, he eased himself from beneath this man, this monstrous devil, who had brought him so close to death.

For a moment he sat with his head

slumped, breathing in long, rasping gasps.

Then, as he regained some composure, he glanced up and saw the girl. She had the gun pointed at him; her eyes filled with insanity. For a long moment the weapon remained levelled, her finger poised on the trigger. He waited. Were all men now branded as enemies to her? He had escaped from death only to be confronted by it again.

At last some seed of understanding must have seeped into her traumatized brain because she allowed the gun to slip from her grasp and drop to the ground.

18

Both Frank and Lucille remained with their heads slumped. The only sound came from the gurgle of water in the gulley. The rain had stopped and the sun was rising. Above them a vivid rainbow arched across the sky.

Frank had saved Lucille's life, and, unbeknown to him, possibly that of her baby as well. In return, she had saved him and in so doing destroyed the evil man who had ruined her life and hopes.

And now Frank had to decide what he must do. The situation was fraught with difficulty. Lucille was so physically weakened by her ordeal that it was unlikely that she would be able to walk. In addition, she was so traumatized that he doubted if she cared whether she lived or died. As for Frank himself, he had lost a good deal of blood, but he had washed the wound clean and he hoped it would heal. Nonetheless his body had taken a severe pummelling and he no longer had the ability to recover quickly as he'd had in his younger days. His throat was constricted and bruised from the throttling it had undergone. And on top of everything, they were marooned in this lonely and forlorn place.

The first idea that came to Frank's mind was prayer, and he knelt on the hard rock, placed his hands together and spoke to the Lord. He didn't plead or beg, but simply asked for divine guidance.

Meanwhile, Lucille appeared to have fallen asleep. He noticed with satisfaction the rise and fall of her chest. He also saw how downright thin she was. It seemed unbelievable that she was the same healthy-looking girl he'd seen in the photograph on Glassner's desk, but he knew she was.

If they were to stand any chance of survival, the responsibility rested on his shoulders. He came to his feet, walked past the corpse of Victorio, about which the flies were now buzzing, and started to climb up the side of the gulley. He came across the place where the kidnappers had made a makeshift campsite. He found a small bundle of rags and on unwrapping it, discovered some stale, mealy bread. He returned to Lucille and roused her. She woke up with suddenness and a look of terror in her eyes. She would have screamed if she'd had sufficient strength. He uttered soothing words, eventually calming her.

He tried to tempt her with the bread but she shook her head. Finally he gave up and gnawed on a crust himself. It was as hard as the rocks.

He hooked his good hand beneath Lucille's armpit and gently dragged her further up the gulley. She made no resistance, and now, at least, she was away from the corpse and the flies that were gathering. Next, he again climbed up the side of the gulley and shortly emerged on a high ridge that was bare save for a scattering of sagebrush and brown grass. He rested for a moment. The sun was already high in the sky, momentarily stupefying him with its brazen heat. A wave of dizziness had him swaying. When he recovered, he gazed out across the Lava Fields, which were shimmering in a haze of steam.

He suspected that his eyes were playing tricks. They saw little bobbing dots in the distance. It's a mirage, he thought. He swallowed hard, watching until his sight became a blur. He blinked, rubbed his brows and refocused his gaze. After a long wait, he saw how the dots were taking the shape of approaching figures ... a group of men, picking their way across the Lava Fields, and he cried out with joy. He thanked the Lord for the salvation that these men would bring. He watched them draw closer.

Fifteen minutes later, he was stumbling down the slope, waving his good arm frantically, attracting the attention of Marshal Colpett, Ben Hardwright

182

and their sweating, eight-man posse.

For their part, they could scarcely believe their good fortune when they saw the fugitive they hunted coming towards them.

★   ★   ★

'Frank Glengarry,' Marshal Colpett said, 'we're arresting you on a charge of murderin' Hector Brampton.'

On reaching the group, Frank had come to a halt. He stood with his legs splayed, believing that his ears were deceiving him. He recognized some of the posse as vigilantes. And with Colpett were his two deputies, Feleen and Buller. They were all staring at him with faces as grim as granite.

'You're what?' Frank gasped.

'You know damn well,' Hardwright cried. The crowd had formed a menacing ring around Frank.

Frank became angry. 'Never mind about me,' he said. 'There's a poor girl back in the gulley — Senator Glassner's daughter. She's been through hell. You'd better get to her before she dies. Close by, you'll find the body of the man who kidnapped her.'

The men surrounding him looked at each other, confused.

One of them said, 'More of his lies. Don't believe a word of it.'

Colpett, however, turned to his deputies and said, 'Go and have a look,' and the two nodded, moved away and clambered up the incline. Soon they disappeared from view.

Hardwright glared at Frank and said, 'I always knew you weren't innocent. If we'd lynched you the first time, we'd have saved the life of Brampton.'

'What are we gonna do with him now?' somebody yelled out.

Another vigilante replied, 'I say we lynch the devil before he does any more murderin' and rapin'.'

A further man said, 'Well there ain't no trees around here. We best lynch him when we find a tree on the way back.'

Marshall Colpett displayed a look of

irritation. 'There'll be no lynchin',' he proclaimed in a voice that nobody could ignore. 'He'll get a fair trial when we get back to town. He'll get justice. Maybe he don't deserve it, but he'll get it!'

At that moment Deputies Feleen and Buller appeared over the ridge and started down towards them. Feleen was carrying the frail girl in his arms.

Frank couldn't understand anything about the crime for which he was being charged. And right now he didn't much care. All that mattered was that they'd be taken back to Modoc Falls.

★　★　★

Firstly, they had the punishing walk back across the Lava Fields, and then they started the journey to where the posse had left their horses. Men took it in turns to carry Lucille, though it was no imposition because she was feather-light. Frank stumbled along under the guard of two vigilantes. It was obvious

185

that he was in too weak a state to attempt escape. Furthermore, he had no intention of doing so. The most important thing to him was to see Lucille safely delivered into caring hands. When they reached the horses, he rode double behind Deputy Buller.

They arrived at the Brampton farm, anxious to see how the poor, grieving widow, who had refused to leave the grave of her husband, had fared.

Colpett was surprised to find the place deserted.

★ ★ ★

Modoc Falls was in a high state of celebration. William 'Cloudburst' Ketchum, the rainmaker, was hailed as a saviour. For the first time in living memory the town's main street had flooded, and children, young folks and dogs had frolicked in the water, and in the Golden Rooster Saloon whiskey was on the house. Out on the ranges as the lakes and streams filled and cattle slaked their thirst, farmers rejoiced and considered that the cash expended to employ the rainmaker had been money well spent. They had no hesitation in paying the balance.

Ketchum himself took full advantage of the goodwill that was awash in the town, spending most of his time in the saloon explaining how bringing on the rain was just a matter of 'seeding' the clouds with fireworks. But the locals said he'd courted the angels.

The rainmaker was draining his glass of 'on-the-house' whiskey, calling it the best tarantula juice he'd ever supped. He told his drinking pals that he was leaving for Boston first thing in the morning. Right then, Fred Pale, one of the vigilantes, came in and spread the word that Frank Glengarry was in the jail and was being charged with the murder of Hector Brampton and the rape of his wife.

Ketchum slopped his whiskey, amazed at the news. 'When did he do that?' he gasped.

'Let me see,' Fred Pale replied. 'Must've been last Tuesday.'

Ketchum just couldn't believe that Glengarry would have committed such a crime. He had come to be downright fond of him during the time they had spent in each other's company. Frank was a God-fearing man and each night he had knelt and said the Lord's Prayer. Furthermore, he'd been doing his utmost to rescue a maiden in distress. Ketchum remembered the conversations with him as they ate supper alongside his campfire, seen the frustration in him as his searching appeared futile.

Ketchum couldn't believe the accusations.

He felt disillusioned.

But he was glad to hear that the girl in question had been found, her kidnapper shot down and that now she was being cared for in the home of Doctor Briggs and his good lady.

He decided he'd done enough drinking, maybe too much. He bade his companions farewell.

'See you next time we have a drought,' Fred Pale said as he left the saloon. 'Don't get lost on the way back to Boston.'

19

So Frank, yet again, was confined in the marshal's jail, the intention being to gather evidence in preparation for a trial by jury. He was relieved when Colpett informed him that the telegraph lines had been restored, and he asked him if he could send a message to his wife.

The marshal nodded and said, 'You write it out. I'll send it for you.'

Frank was supplied with pencil and paper and he jotted down a message to Rebecca, apologizing for not communicating previously. He did his best to reassure her, saying that his mission had taken longer than anticipated, but that the kidnapped girl was now rescued. He told Rebecca he was well and prayed for her every night, and that he missed her and loved her with all his heart. He didn't mention that he was awaiting trial and might get the death penalty. She would only worry.

Frank related to Colpett his experiences. He informed him where the bodies of Jim Esthelder and Victorio were, and the marshal said that he would send men out to bring them in. Frank then mentioned his suspicion that there was a haversack of cash somewhere close to the gulley where the girl had been found. Colpett said he would go out with his men and attend to the matter personally.

★   ★   ★

William Ketchum was pretty well oiled when he retired to his hotel bed late that night, but not so much that his brain wasn't still ticking over. He was still absorbing the news of Glengarry's guilt. Around 1 a.m. reality hit him. Frank couldn't have committed the murder on Tuesday, as Fred Pale had claimed, because he was with him in the mountains right then.

Next morning, Ketchum, completely sober now, took an early breakfast. He had decided to postpone his return to Boston, at least for a few hours. Soon he contacted Marshal Colpett and explained the situation to him. Colpett advised Ketchum to go to the local lawyer and take out an affidavit, swearing that Glengarry was with him at the time of the murder so could not have been guilty.

Ketchum gladly complied.

Three days later, after much consultation, Frank was released from jail and all charges were dropped.

Senator Glassner was informed that his daughter had been freed and that her condition was most poorly. He immediately despatched a doctor and nurse to bring her home. They arrived within the week.

Frank accompanied them on their return journey to Texas, by rail and stage, sleeping much of the time and hoping that Lucille would react to kind treatment. But she remained completely unresponsive. Even when she was told of Jim Esthelder's death she showed no emotion.

20

Lucille's eyes remained pools of blankness, always gazing to the front. She bore little resemblance to the vibrant young girl who had been out riding on the fateful day of her kidnap. Her pregnancy was developing. It was a miracle that the baby had survived, despite all she had suffered. Perhaps it was due to the strong constitution the baby inherited from his father. Lucille took no interest in her condition. It was if she had disowned her swollen belly.

Wilber Glassner was fully occupied in Washington but he still found time to write to his daughter regularly and he was greatly relieved that she had been freed and that any scandal appeared to have been kept under wraps. Lucille scanned through his letters but showed no reaction to them and it was not clear whether she understood the words or not. Glassner was very grateful to Frank and Rebecca Glengarry, who had taken his daughter into their home and lavished upon her the gentle, forgiving ways of the Hanna Church.

Frank heard that Marshal Colpett had recovered the cash from where it had been placed by Victorio close to the gulley in which he'd died. Colpett had returned it through banking channels to Glassner. Frank had always considered him an honest man and was glad to learn that he'd kept his job as town marshal.

Each week, Doctor Crabtree examined Lucille, constantly seeking improvement in her condition. He said he was hopeful, and that he had seen patients who had undergone similar ordeals, mainly women who had been captured by the Comanches. They had recovered and afterwards led comparatively normal lives. After rescue, some had even given birth to babies sired by Indian fathers. But the months slipped by with no change.

Every reassurance in the world could not lift Lucille from her torpid state. All she could manage was an occasional nod or shake of the head. Frank wondered if he would ever live to see the day when she smiled. Nonetheless, he and Rebecca bestowed limitless love and care on her and every night prayed that she would become well.

Frank's wound gradually healed, but, like Lucille, he had suffered terrible tribulation, and sometimes, he would cry out in his sleep as his dreams revisited his experiences. It was as if a curtain was drawn back from his memory and he was again on the threshold of being lynched, or he was gazing once more into the black borehole of Victorio's gun. But always Rebecca was there to soothe him as he awoke, her gentle words and faith in the Lord bringing him back to a world in which he no longer had to face death at every turn. Over the months his mind gradually regained some of its old serenity and many bad memories slid into the background.

But as Frank mulled over past events, he came to an alarming realization.

He'd seen Brampton's corpse when he'd been returning to the Lava Fields several days before Blanche told the members of the posse that her husband had been murdered 'the day before yesterday'. The two didn't tie together. The truth was that he might have had the opportunity to kill Brampton if he hadn't been dead already. Ketchum had sworn an affidavit in good faith, but if Blanche had given the correct date of her husband's death, the murder charge against Frank might have stood. For sure, he thought uneasily, it might still stand!

Anxiety rose in him when a Pinkerton detective, whom he did not know, arrived at the farmhouse in Marion County.

★　★　★

Before this, dramatic events had taken place in Nevada. On rushing from the First National Bank, Blanche Brampton had gone to the Winnemucca Hotel where she was staying. She knew she had to make tracks fast. She just couldn't understand how her 'fortune' had been proved fraudulent, but she knew she was in no position to dispute it. Before leaving the hotel, she was presented with a bill by the proprietor. She paid this from the small supply of the worthless bills she had left. She hastened to the Union Pacific railroad station where she paid for her ticket, again with the fake money. After that, all her cash was gone, but she told herself that the most important thing was to travel to as distant a place as possible. She was gutted by events. She would be broke when she got there; however, maybe fate would turn up something.

But the train wasn't due out for a couple of hours and she waited in the car, fuming at the delay.

At the same time police officers had traced her to the hotel. On arrival they informed the proprietor that the lady in question was using forged money. The money with which she'd paid her bill was checked and forgery confirmed. By the time the train left Winnemucca, police officers had suspected the means by which she was leaving and sent a telegraph message to the marshal in the small township of Elko.

He boarded the car when it stopped. It didn't take him long to identify the big lady in fine clothes.

Blanche strove to avoid arrest. She struggled with the marshal in the aisle of the car and, with her immense strength, would have overpowered him had she not had the misfortune to trip over a spittoon. As she fell, he lashed her across the face with ungentlemanly force, stunning her. By that time a fellow passenger had come to the aid of the law officer. Together, they subdued her and the marshal snapped handcuffs on to her thick wrists.

Over the following week she was interrogated by law officers and she grew furious at their persistence, attempted violence and being restrained. She eventually told a fabricated story that her husband had stolen the money from Frank Glengarry.

★   ★   ★

When the Pinkerton detective visited him, Frank feared that he was about to be arrested and charged with the murder of Hector Brampton, but such was not the case. The detective took down a long statement and Frank related his entire experience.

During the following month, the investigation widened. Senator Wilber Glassner was consulted and he gave evidence with a plea that the case was not to be publicized. In view of the delicate state of events, the authorities agreed. Marshal Colpett was also interviewed at Modoc Falls. When all evidence was accrued, Blanche Brampton was not only charged with passing fraudulent money, but also with the murder of her husband. Seething with fury, she told the jury at her trial to 'take the high road to hell' and that *of course* she had murdered her mouse of a husband! She said that if they weren't so utterly stupid, they'd have realized that from the start.

Some time after the conviction, the news of the trial found itself reported in the *Travis Springs Gazette.*

Mrs Blanche Brampton, a former resident of the Modoc Falls district, California, has been found guilty of murder.

Frank breathed a sigh of relief; he would never forget sitting at a table with the Bramptons and wondering if the stew he was eating was poisoned.

Lucille gave birth to a son at the expected time, finding her voice at last as she cried out with birth pangs. At first she wanted nothing to do with the child, thrusting him aside from her breast. She at last mouthed a word . . . 'Monster!' But Rebecca coaxed her with unremitting patience, and, three weeks on, there came a breakthrough. One morning a light came into Lucille's eyes, her lips widened into a faint smile and she whispered, 'My baby. Pretty baby. Jim's baby.' And she took it in her arms and showed the first glimmer of happiness that they had seen.

And then it struck Frank . . . *Jim's baby*.

Lucille had realized something he had overlooked. *The resemblance!* As the days slipped by it became more and more noticeable. The blue eyes, the blonde hair, the little nose and chin.

Of course, before her kidnapping, Lucille would never have revealed to her father the intimate relationship she'd shared with the young wheelwright. But now it became clear that she had given birth to Jim Esthelder's son, not that of her persecutor, and as her traumatized mind absorbed this fact, everything seemed to change.

Thus began her long journey back towards a semblance of normality, a journey during which her father, William Glassner, paid several visits. He was magnanimous, once again expressing his profound gratitude to Frank and Rebecca and proclaiming love and sympathy for his daughter. He never questioned the paternity of his grandson. He even held him in his arms, albeit clumsily.

He invited Frank and Rebecca to his inauguration, in Washington, as President of the United States, but they declined the offer as they believed that folks dressed in simple Hanna costume would be out of place amongst all the dignitaries in their top hats.

And so their lives slipped back to the pastoral tranquillity they had known in the past, disturbed only by the cries of Lucille's little boy as he grew into a sturdy toddler. Frank knew that the

Lord had sorely tested him, and he had not failed, although the cost had been high. He promised Rebecca that he would never come out of retirement again.

THE END

We do hope that you have enjoyed reading this large print book.

Did you know that all of our titles are available for purchase?

We publish a wide range of high quality large print books including:
Romances, Mysteries, Classics
General Fiction
Non Fiction and Westerns

Special interest titles available in large print are:
The Little Oxford Dictionary
Music Book, Song Book
Hymn Book, Service Book

Also available from us courtesy of Oxford University Press:
Young Readers' Dictionary
(large print edition)
Young Readers' Thesaurus
(large print edition)

For further information or a free brochure, please contact us at:
Ulverscroft Large Print Books Ltd.,
The Green, Bradgate Road, Anstey,
Leicester, LE7 7FU, England.
Tel: (00 44) **0116 236 4325**
Fax: (00 44) **0116 234 0205**

THE HONOUR OF THE BADGE

Scott Connor

US Marshal Stewart Montague was a respected mentor to young Deputy Lincoln Hawk, guiding his first steps as a lawman and impressing upon him the importance of the honour of the badge. Twenty years later, the pair are pursuing a gang of bandits when Montague goes missing, presumed murdered. For six months, Hawk continues the mission alone, without success. But when he stumbles into the gang's hideout, there is a great shock in store. Seems his old companion isn't six feet under after all . . .

RETURN OF THE BANDIT

Roy Patterson

Villainous bounty hunter Hume Crawford is well-known for his brutal slayings: he will do anything to get his hands on those he seeks. Out to find and kill the legendary bandit Zococa, despite reports of the good-natured rogue's death, Crawford proceeds to shoot his way across the Mexican border. But he has attracted the attention of Marshal Hal Gunn and his deputy Toby Jones. As Crawford follows Zococa's trail, there are two Texas star riders on his . . .

THE PHANTOM STRIKES

Walt Keene

The desert terrain was once haunted by the Phantom — a blanched man on a pale-grey horse, who struck in the night and killed without mercy. Wild Bill Hickock shot the legend down once — and twenty years later, when the Phantom's son took up the torch, he did so again . . . With both culprits dead, Hickock and his compadres are satisfied they have laid the ghost to rest. But when a mortally wounded man gasps that the spirit has returned, they must take up arms once more — against the Phantom's second son . . .

THE BRONC BUSTER

Billy Hall

Tormented by a fearsome gang because of his small stature, fourteen-year-old Ian Hennessy swears one day never to run from anyone again. Years later, as the young bronc buster stares down a gunfighter, there is no doubt that his old enemy — Shaunnessy O'Toole, ringleader of his childhood bullies — is behind it. Meanwhile, a second man lurks nearby, also poised to shoot. All Hennessy's dreams — establishing a ranch, marrying the girl he loves — hang in the balance of this moment . . .